HERE FOR IT

ERIN MARIE BASSETT

Published by EMB MKT, LLC
Copyright 2023
Cover Design by Erin Marie Bassett

www.erinmariebassett.com

ISBN: 9798860460355

For Danny, my first and lasting love.

PROLOGUE

KYLE

"Kyle! How was the interview? Tell me everything."

"Yeah hi, uh, Mom."

Wait.

That girl is really cute.

Our eyes connected as she quickly smiled at me then passed by walking into the lobby. No, it was more like she bounced into the lobby. Her eyes were round and dark but they sparkled and I never really noticed hair on a girl before but hers was a shiny chestnut color that seemed to flow along with the sway of her hips. I couldn't help myself from checking her out once she passed me and I can say with certainty that her hips sway rather nicely.

"Kyle? You there?"

Oh yeah, I'm on the phone with Mom. Stop thinking about a girl's butt. I clear my throat.

"Yeah, I'm here. Hi. The interview was good. They seemed nice and the conversation was, urm, good."

Was that her laugh? Shit, it's a melody. I'm moving in slow motion across the lobby as I continue looking over my shoulder in her direction.

"I hope you were more eloquent during the interview." My mom says with a laugh.

"I was. I could tell they were impressed by Aunt Mary's recommendation too." I reach the door and step back to hold it open for someone walking into the building, giving me one last chance to sneak a peek at the cute girl. "Hopefully that hel---oh shit!"

I hear my mom gasping "What! What happened?" into the phone as I watch the really cute girl completely wipe out. Ski slope yard sale wipe out.

Her bag slides across the polished marble floor to the right, one of her shoes to the left. She stands up and looks horrified. Instinctively I took a few steps in her direction before I realized that I'm already out of the security gate and all I can do is look on and watch from a distance. She takes a hand from a guy old enough to be her grandpa. She does a little thank you bow to the man who hands her back her shoe. She slips it on while she hops on the other foot and kind of laughs and says "Well they better give me the job now!" as she taps the elevator button urgently and tries to hide her face behind her hair as she waits.

I'm brought back to my phone call by Mom yelling "Kyle! What is going on!?" and, with one last look back as the elevator doors open for her, I tell my mom what I just witnessed as I make my way out the door to the sidewalk.

"Oh, poor little thing."

All I could think about was how cute she looked during the whole damn mess.

CHAPTER 1

KYLE

My feet pound to a halt at the corner of my building. I'm glad I took my cousin Bryan's advice to start my day with a run or a workout. I put on some weight during the last few months of grad school. Between the late nights, fast food, and celebratory nights out my workout routine took a back seat. I've been running in the morning since I moved to the city a few weeks ago and it feels really fucking good. I'm energized throughout the day and feel the good kind of tired at night.

My internship with Fosters, Henderson and Associates starts today. From everything I've heard it is boring and stressful and the company culture is stiff and unwelcoming. Can't wait. But my Aunt Mary has promised to hire me at her foundation, YouthFull, once I have some experience somewhere else under my belt. Fine, I guess that's fair. I just want to get through the next 8 weeks, turn down the job they'll most likely offer me, because I'm smart and a hard worker, not cocky, and get started designing the Summer Camp for YF.

Once I'm upstairs in my apartment I have a glass of water then take a shower and put on the suit my mom bought me for the interview for this job. The day when that cute girl wiped out in the lobby. I think about her at least once a day. How she smiled after she fell. How she balanced her bag in the crook of her elbow as she slipped on her shoe and also pushed the hair out of her face. Does she work in the building? Was she just there for a meeting? Will I see her again? What are the chances?

After my interview I took the train back up to Yale and met up with my buddies at our favorite bar, Ordinary. It wasn't where we hung out as underclassmen but as sophisticated Graduate students we leveled up our going out game. When I sat down at our high top table Jeff asked me how the interview went and he was satisfied with my answer of "good" so I didn't have to get into telling him about the girl that crashed and burned in the lobby. No, that was the story I told to him a few hours later when I was reminded of her when a girl with brown hair like hers walked into the bar. Another hour after that Jeff had introduced me to that girl with brown hair, Tiffany, and we've been hooking up ever since. She just graduated and her job in the city starts in a few weeks so she's back home in Florida until then. We text, and sext, but honestly most of the time I forget I'm dating someone. We just don't get into anything substantial.

I'm not sure I could tell you what her favorite color is. Or confirm the number of siblings she has. One? Three? Or maybe they're her cousins.

I don't think she could answer those things about me either.

It's zero siblings by the way, only child here, but a close knit group of five cousins.

One of those cousins is Bryan who is an executive coach and five years older. He has been giving me a lot of life advice about starting this job because Aunt Mary is his mom and he knows what she'll be wanting from me when I start at YF. He's got the career thing locked down but still hasn't found a long-term girlfriend. Not that I'm following his lead but if he doesn't have one yet I'm in no rush to have one myself.

I'll have to ask him to recommend a podcast to listen to while I walk to work because thinking about life timelines probably isn't the healthiest.

Fosters, Henderson and Associates is located in a large office building on Lexington Ave, the Graybar building. The Chrysler Building is across the street. I'm not impressed by historic landmarks. I don't care if this building is considered prestigious. They're just places where work gets done.

What's good about the location is that there are a ton of different lunch places, coffee shops, delis and bodegas nearby. And I only live a few blocks down in Murray Hill. I'm a little early for the first day so I stop for an iced coffee across the street from the office. We got an email telling us all to meet Judy, the intern coordinator, in the lobby at 8am. In my house, arriving on time meant you were late, so at 7:45 I come through the revolving doors to find three people standing in a group and I see Judy is one of them.

"Good morning." Judy greets me without much emotion. Already seeming stressed before the day has started. The two other interns kind of nod and respond with murmured "mornings" and while I'm not the most outgoing person in the world I'm also bummed this group seems so subdued.

"I'm Kyle Sutherland." I say to the group with a wave and a smile.

"Nora Heely" and she holds out her hand to shake.

"Hey man, Chandler Ashforth" and he holds out his fist for knuckles.

The four of us stand around not saying anything and it is awkward. Judy is scanning the lobby with a disapproving look on her face. After a few minutes she checks her watch and says "I guess we'll just wait here a few more minutes for our last intern to arri-"

She's cut short when I bump into her because someone bumped into me. I turn around and can't believe my eyes. It's Lobby Girl! She has her phone and a travel coffee mug in one hand and as she steps back her bag slides down from her shoulder to her elbow which sets her off kilter again. She adjusts it with a hop, pushes her hair out of her face, and looks up at me.

"Oh gosh! Sorry! Hi-ii I'm Liz!" and her tone is cheerful, perky, and refreshing.

"And, this is Liz." Judy says by way of introduction. "Liz, meet Nora, Chandler and Kyle. Okay, follow me to get your badges." I hold out my arm in an "after you" gesture and I enjoy seeing her smile as she steps past.

"Here is the copier, fax machine and binding machine. You'll be using these quite a bit over the next eight weeks. And through here," we all follow

Judy who is moving at a swift clip through the hallway but stops at a conference room at the end of the hall, "is where you'll be working."

The one wall of windows look straight into another office building full of cubicles and fluorescent lights. It can't be more than eight feet away. Most of the room's square footage is occupied by one big oval table with four laptops and a speaker phone sitting on it in the middle.

"Nice view." Chander says in a barely masked sarcastic tone.

"Indeed." Jody replies curtly before continuing. "You'll each have a laptop to use for your work and you've been given Fosters email addresses. In a little bit, Toby, our technical assistant will come in to help you get set up. After that we have a meeting with Deb, our office manager, followed by orientation with Patricia from HR. She'll be reviewing the Fosters Code of Conduct. Then we'll break for a 30 minute lunch before you are assigned to your teams and meet with them to receive your first assignments."

Liz is standing at the front of our little foursome and she raises her hand.

"Yes?" Judy says annoyed.

"Where is the bathroom?"

"Back down the hall to the left. You'll need the code, 781."

"781. Got it. Be right back!" She unceremoniously sets her bag, coffee mug, and phone on the table. When she pivots to leave she is facing me because I've made a point to stand behind her or next to her for this whole tour. She gives me another smile before sliding past me and out of the conference room down the hall.

"Well there's no use continuing until she is back. Please take your seats and Toby should be here soon."

CHAPTER 2

LIZ

Okay, Fosters, I see you. This is a nice bathroom. And at this point in my day I'll take whatever I can get because so far it has not gone as planned. And by plan I mean it hasn't matched the perfect movie version of my first day of work as a bonafide grown up.

The movie version I played in my head as I went to bed last night went something like this:

A polished, chipper 20-something, rises before her alarm and chuckles to herself because she's so responsible that she didn't need her alarm in the first place. She slips into a silk robe and goes to turn on the shower. She plays her favorite personal growth podcast while she showers. After wrapping her hair in a microfiber towel she brews herself an artisan cup of pour over coffee and enjoys it while standing in front of her quiet luxury wardrobe of neutral but high end pieces, which are immaculately organized, to select an outfit for the day.

I'll start by saying that my hair is still wet. Oh, and I slept through my alarm. There's a ginormous stress zit on my chin that decided to move in overnight and I dropped my mascara onto my white shirt this morning so I had to find another shirt to wear. Which is easier said than done because I moved in over the weekend and didn't prioritize unpacking my work clothes fast enough so they're all wrinkled.

Now, I'm sweating through my second blouse of the day because one, I'm riled up, two, I was basically a sardine on the train this morning, and three, and here's the big one, one of my fellow interns is a total hunk.

When I skidded into the lobby, at 7:57, which was not technically late but I was still the last one there, I ran smack into Hunky McShoulders and his one-sided-dimple smile. The look in his blue eyes was amused and surprised so I don't think he was too bothered by my hot mess express arrival.

Then he has stood either right next to or right behind me during our whole little office tour and I am feeling cute-boy flustered in addition to first-job flustered.

With my bladder empty and my armpits dabbed with hand towels, I head back into the conference room and notice that Chandler and Kyle (McShoulders) are on one side of the table and Nora is on the other. Observing middle school dance rules I take a seat next to Nora but now I'm forced to look directly at Kyle and his adorable face.

To try and busy my hands so I don't fidget in front of my new peers slash competition. I gather up my bag and phone and coffee mug and move it under the table in front of me. Then I text a picture of my work badge to my dad. He's less excited about this internship than I am. Ever practical, he has been on constant budget patrol because this internship isn't paid. At the end of the summer Fosters offer full time positions to the top interns meaning I have the next eight weeks to knock their socks off.

Professional fundraising has been my targeted career ever since I learned it was a thing. Which was when I was a freshman at Brown. My roommate was in a scientific research class and started telling me about how research projects get funded. And how important public and corporate grants and nonprofits were. After that I became fascinated by the whole system. I might not have the brains for doing the research but I could easily persuade people to fund it.

Landing this internship is the first step on the path to that career. Everything in the Collins home is about career paths. Since my siblings are 11 and 8 years older than I am I've had a lot of discussions around college, major selection, and ultimate career path.

Charlie Jr, but don't call him CJ, my older brother went the doctor route, graduated from Dartmouth for undergrad and med school, after a residency in Los Angeles, he's back home. Well sort of. He's the head of the Emergency Department at the regional hospital near our hometown.

Margaret, my older sister, went the lawyer route and just graduated from Harvard Law with her JD.

Little ole Liz just graduated, all wide eyed and bushy tailed, and she couldn't tell her dad exactly what she was going to be now that she was a grown up. It was a painful conversation at Spring Break. But I was able to mollify him and explain that in order to be a professional fundraiser I'd need to work for a few years and gain experience. There aren't really college degrees for this specifically. Maybe eventually I'll move into public policy or have my own consulting firm.

Actually, that's the dream. My own firm where I can have a team of people to do the boring administrative tasks, and people who will do my hair, makeup, and wardrobe selections for me and call it a business expense.

My mind is focused on the vision of me sitting at a vanity getting my hair blown out while I tap away on my phone doing important business when Judy walks back into the room with a skinny guy wearing thick rimmed black glasses. I hate that he's the stereotypical tech guy but he is. So high school AV club. Which, don't get me wrong, is an important club to be a part of, those people learn real skills, but arguably not the coolest one to belong to. Not that I was cool in high school but I hope my art kid crowd had a leg up on the AV kids.

He walks us through setting passwords and getting us logged into the group chat platform. He finishes up and leaves us as Judy walks back in.

"You'll only be able to email internally during your internship. Our clients know we have you working on their projects but you won't have the opportunity to work directly with them unless you're hired at the end of the summer. Your job will be to support the Partners and Consultants with whatever they need."

Judy gets called out of the room for a phone call. Nora stage whispers "this feels like detention" to me and we all giggle.

"I've been to plenty of detentions, this one has the best view." Chandler, who has the look of prep school golden boy about him says as he eyes Nora. "Should we try to do actual introductions while she's gone?"

"Sure, I'll go first. I'm Nora Heely, from New Jersey. My favorite drink is iced coffee, spiked if necessary, and I'm hoping to get the gig because I want to go into higher education fundraising and Fosters has some of the most prestigious schools on their client roster."

"Will it sounds like AA if we all say 'Hi Nora' together?" Chandler supplies.

"Ha, probably, I'll just go next then. Hi," I insert a quick wave, "I'm Liz Collins. I'm from Lakeville, NY which is upstate and really small. My favorite drink is also iced coffee but if we're talking booze then I'm a gin and tonic gal. I want the Fosters job because I want to have a career where I'm helping the people who, well, help the people."

"Is that what you said in your interview?" asks Hunky McShoulders, aka Kyle, and I can't tell if he's being sassy or just unanimated.

"No, I was able to put together better sentences for the interview." I say with sass but refrain from sticking out my tongue. I wasn't really looking to divulge my interview proposals and I didn't like the challenge in his voice. I did not stick my tongue out at him but I was tempted to.

Before Kyle can respond, or he and Chandler do their introductions, Judy marches back in with a cheerful looking woman in tow.

"Interns, this is Deb. She is our office manager. She is who you'll work with if you need supplies ordered or there's an issue with any of the copy machines."

"Hello Deb!" I say with a wave and while Deb smiles at me Judy seems to shoot daggers in my direction.

"Hi everyone, if you'd please follow me to the copy room I'll show you some basics. Always feel free to ask me for help if you're feeling lost or stumped. I'd rather help than have a broken machine to deal with." Deb says kindly before she turns and walks out of the room.

"Our dress policy is an important one to follow. No, you will not be interacting with clients during your internship but at Fosters we believe in putting your best foot forward always. On the off chance a client visits our office we need to make a perfect impression. You'll see on page 48 that a list of unacceptable clothing items is provided." Patricia says over her reading glasses that perch perilously at the end of her nose. "Are there any questions?"

We all glance up at each other and shake our heads no. I mean, my hopes of wearing cute maxi dresses under blazers this summer is out the window because it says here that no flowy dresses or floor length skirts are allowed. Nor are open toed shoes or sandals. I knew Fosters was a serious place but this feels super outdated and kind of sexist. Like most of the items listed on the prohibited list are things women would wear.

"Okay, if there are no questions you're free to leave for lunch. Please be back by 12:30. Your meetings with the Partners begin at 1." Judy says as she snaps the elastic around her notebook, stands, and leaves the room.

"Anyone want to see what that deli across the street has for lunch?" Chandler asks as we push back our chairs.

"I stopped in there for a coffee earlier, it seems like a good spot." Kyle offers.

"I'm game, Liz?" Nora says, looking at me.

"I haven't found a deli serving bagels and coffee that I don't like so count me in."

The four of us make our way down through the lobby and across the street. The deli is busy but I can already tell it's going to be exactly what I need. I order an iced coffee with a sesame bagel sandwich with turkey, tomatoes and lettuce and make my way to the end of the counter to wait for my food. Nora orders next and shortly after Kyle and Chandler join us.

"Since we got cut off earlier, allow me to introduce myself. I'm Chandler Ashforth. I grew up here. I got this internship because my dad told me to and you're all invited out to our place in the Hamptons next weekend while my parents are in Nantucket for a wedding."

"Ooo yes please! I'm in." I say while greedily rubbing my hands together. I notice a smirk from McShoulders. Does he find me amusing?

"Same." Nora adds with a sip of her iced coffee.

"Sounds fun man, thanks. I'm Kyle Sutherland, I grew up in Connecticut and I got this internship to get some experience before going to work for my aunt who runs the YouthFull Foundation in the Bronx. She didn't want to hire me straight out of school but we came up with this idea for a summer camp last Christmas and once this internship is over I'm headed there to help get it up and running."

"That's so cool!" Maybe if I act super excited I won't come across as insanely jealous because the list of what I wouldn't give to have a family connection like that is really short. "I've heard of YouthFull. My friend did an observation there for one of our public policy courses. She said Mary, who I guess is your Aunt, built the whole program from nothing and now they help like a thousand kids a week!"

"It's more like two thousand." Kyle clarifies. Okay, fine, be precise. "And yeah. She started out as a high school English teacher and realized that a lot of her students were struggling to complete assignments outside of school. They either didn't have good homes to go to or they had to work after school jobs. So she started an after school tutoring club and it grew from there. Now it's academics, sports, arts, and sciences. It's awesome."

"That's very cool. Now," Nora says as she takes a bite of her sandwich, "what sectors do you hope to get assigned to? I'm hoping for Higher Education. Give me some alumni and some five year plans!"

"I could care less." Chandler says while giving a girl who just walked in a once over. I'm surprised he even took the time to answer the question he's so locked in to her.

"It's not that I don't care, it just doesn't really matter to me since I'm going to YF after this." Kyle says while reaching past me to grab a napkin.

"I really want medical and life sciences. I think there is so much potential for public policy support in those areas and I want to help our clients partner with the public sector to maximize their impact." I share. And although my true passion lies in the arts and graphic design and being a professional photographer is the ultimate dream, this is the practical choice. There will always be hospitals looking for more money. There will always be labs looking to develop the next big pharmaceutical. And even if I don't get the job at the end of the internship, which would be a total blow to my ego, I'm hoping to gain enough experience to pitch myself to other organizations.

"Knowing what my aunt has had to deal with on the public policy side I'm not sure non-profits and the government play nicely together. There's too much red tape stopping the people who want to make a real difference."

Oooo-kay. So there's a chip on Hunky McShoulder's, well, hunky shoulders. And the way he said that makes me feel like he's challenging me or doubting me and as a result my defensive walls go up. I arm my weapons.

Which are my wit and sense of humor, obviously.

Lucky for me I've put some thought into this. Fosters asked the interns to prepare a case study to present during our interviews. Confidence isn't usually something I lack so I marched, heck I almost skipped, into the lobby for my interview armed with the knowledge that while the data I presented in my case study wasn't ground breaking, the way I presented it was. My marketing and public policy double majors worked right alongside my graphic design and photography minors. A perfect blend of red tape and poetry. I used my design skills to put together an animated presentation for how a women's hospital could not only attract younger donors but use the data about their current donors to set the goals.

I had rehearsed my presentation, I had an extra printed copy and my digital copy was backed up and downloaded. Tablet charged. Connector cables packed in case they wanted me to use a projector. My outfit was the almost never attained trifecta of polished, current, and comfortable. I was early. Everything was coming up Lizzard. And then I wiped out in the lobby.

Embarrassed barely begins to describe how I felt but I rallied, landed a joke on the old guy who helped me up. (After he said "Oof, that's gotta hurt." Jackass.) And was able to not just get through the interview but do well enough to get an offer.

Remembering what I went through that day gives me a boost of confidence.

"Well maybe they just need a better recess monitor to help them play nicely together." I say while I take the last bite of my sandwich and drop a piece of tomato on my skirt.

Well, shit.

CHAPTER 3

KYLE

The first three days at Fosters have gone pretty well. Liz and I are assigned to Medical Sciences together, Chandler got the Arts and Nora got Higher Ed like she wanted. Our first meeting with Marcus Linard and Lauren Gill, the MedSci partners, went fine but Liz and I failed to ask one important question.

"What will we be doing day-to-day?"

Because what we are doing is boring AF.

The tasks are menial and definitely could be automated if Fosters invested in some technology. But then again they wouldn't be able to offer this 'chance of a lifetime' internship. Chandler creates little games for himself. Nora plops on a playlist and focuses on her paperwork. Liz and I stumble through who is going to do what. She is oddly competitive about the task assignments. I wouldn't classify myself as a laid back person but her level of investment in this makes me feel particularly laissez faire.

Today, for example, we are assembling reports for a meeting early next week.

"Okay, Kyle, so I think what makes the most sense is for one of us to create and print the cover pages on the cover weight paper while the other person lines up the binding components."

"Sure, sounds good."

"Or should one person do both of those things since they're already in the copy room?"

"That works too."

"Okay, let's do that then. One person creates the cover, prints it, and while it's printing they can pull the coils and backs."

"So, do you want to—"

"Or, actually, one person should create the cover page and then the other person print it. Then the first person can start to assemble the reports."

"Alright. So do you—"

"Nope, let's go back. Okay so one person does the covers while the other starts to get the pieces together and then we'll meet back in the conference room to start assembling."

"Who is goin—"

"Oh shit! I forgot that we need to punch the holes in the reports before we do the binding."

As much fun as I'm having with this display of her timid confidence we're not going to get anything done if she keeps debating with herself.

"Liz?"

"Yeah?"

"I'm going to start punching holes in the reports. You create the cover page and print it. If you get done with that then you can pull the coils and back sheets and we'll finish binding them together."

"Okay. Cool."

I'm actually looking forward to working together on the reports because I'm excited to hang with her. She's smart and talkative. Mostly because she speaks in this stream-of-consciousness way where she questions her gut instinct but then goes with it anyway after debating with herself.

Plus she is energetic. She hasn't been late but she's always rushing in at the last minute and plopping in her chair less than a minute before Judy marches in to give us the morning update. And she does things like drop pens on her lap and ends up with marks on her skirts. Pencil skirts that hug her shapely bottom half. Not that I've noticed. Much.

Once I'm finished stacking the 20 copies with their holes punched on the conference room table, I decide to grab some water from the break room. Liz's back is turned to me while she is waiting for the coffee machine to finish. She's swaying from side to side and I have to think about looking away from her ass. I clear my throat quickly.

"Hey, I just finished the copies and they're ready for the covers."

"Awesome. I'll load the cardstock paper into the machine right after my hot bean water is ready."

I chuckle. It's things like that, calling coffee 'hot bean water', that make her so much fun to hang around with. I wonder if she has friends in the city. If she has a roommate. A boyfriend? I was lucky enough to get an apartment in Murray Hill as a sublet from Bryan because otherwise I'd be living with my buddy Jeff in Brooklyn. My parents are helping with rent before my job starts at YF.

She turns towards me with the mug in her hands and leans back against the counter clutching it to her chest. And, I've gotta admit, I like her chest as much as I like her ass.

"I can't believe this job is making copies. And pulling data, printing spreadsheets, copy editing, printing reports, binding them, shipping them. Ugggghhh we're paper pushers and I don't know how I'm going to last 7 more weeks here. Especially with Micro B needing to be updated on ev-er-y-thing."

I nod and laugh a little. We've given our intern coordinator, Judy, the nickname Micro B because she has her nose in everything we're doing. Like we can't send emails to other Fosters employees unless she reads them first. Thankfully we created an intern only group text so we can communicate without her involvement.

"It feels like such a waste of time and energy. And honestly I'm surprised she's not in here telling me how to make my coffee." Liz continues and I'm about to respond when Judy walks by the break room.

"Oh, there you are Liz. Can you make sure that the report for Donald is printed and bound by the time you go home tonight? He'll need it shipped to his hotel tomorrow so it's ready to go on Monday."

"Yep, Kyle and I are on it."

I toss up a little wave to Judy who grimaces and walks away.

Together we exchange a look of exasperation and then make our way to the conference room. Our hand-me-down laptops are fighting for table space with the printed reports stacked on the table. I watch in slow motion as Liz's heel gets caught on one of the cords and she begins to teeter towards the table.

"Shit!" Liz hisses as she rights herself and looks down at the coffee that has sloshed out of the mug and onto her shirt. "Well, thankfully there's no harm done to the electronics, or the reports, but this shirt is a goner."

Without a word, I jog back to the break room for some paper towels. She follows behind me down the hall holding out her coffee soaked shirt. When I hand her the paper towels my eye catches on her lacy bra that is now outlined under her coffee soaked shirt. I think she notices me checking her out because she's looking at me when my eyes flicker back up to her face.

"Okay, got it Universe, message received, coffee too late in the day is a bad idea."

With a laugh we both turn to head back to the conference room. My hand instinctively falls to the small of her back and I hear her quick intake of breath. And while I would gladly leave my fingers there gently brushing her skin through her shirt I pull back quickly. My hand hits my thigh with an audible the *thump*.

I clear my throat. "So the reports are all done. If you want to start the cover pages I'll start punching the holes in the clear covers. Do you know if Donald likes glossy or matte?"

"No clue. My gut tells me it's glossy. He seems like a fancy fella."

"Ha okay, let's go with glossy then."

"Slap." Liz replies.

"What?"

"Ha oh sorry, that's something my roommate and I used to say to each other. SLAP, Sounds Like A Plan."

"I like it."

"There's plenty more where that came from Sutherland. Stick with me and you'll be abbreviating things like a pro in no time."

"Something to add to my LinkedIn profile."

"Totally." She says with chuckle and then she moves to her laptop to print the cover sheets.

CHAPTER 4

LIZ

Shit. Shit. Shit. Shit. Fuckity shit.

There's a typo on the cover sheet.

We're halfway through binding these freaking reports and I just noticed it. I'm surprised Kyle didn't already; he's sharp and detail oriented. He's gonna be so annoyed. It's already after six because apparently it takes 15 minutes to bind each report and paying, I don't know, a professional printing service to do this is too much to ask. Not when there's free intern labor to be had.

"Soooo, don't hate me."

"Why would I hate you?" He says as he looks up at me with his clear blue eyes.

"Well I just noticed that," pause for effect "there's a typo on the cover sheet."

"What! Where?"

"Donald is spelled wrong."

"No way." Kyle looks at the cover of the report he just finished binding. "Oh shit, yeah it is."

Instead of it saying Donald Nicholls it says Danold Nicholls.

Kyle takes a deep breath. I prepare myself for a lashing. For Kyle to say 'well you screwed this up so you can fix it' because that's honestly what I deserve in a situation like this. For him to bail and leave me to fix this all on my own. It's only fair. I better get a few more granola bars from the break room for dinner.

"Okay, this is fine. We'll fix it and print new ones. While you do that I'll start to cut the binding off of the ones we've already done."

Wait, what?

I just stare at him because if this were the other way around and the person I had been working with had screwed up like this and we needed to redo hours of work I'd probably scream. Well no I wouldn't, I'm too nice. I'd scream in my head and then offer to re-do it all for them in a friendly but also passive aggressive way.

I cannot believe I made this mistake. I do this kind of thing all the time. I notice so many details but the one that matters slips through my grasp. I got dinged on a college paper once for forgetting to put one quote from the 50 pages into the appendix. No matter how hard I try I'm never perfect.

"Hey." He says softly, pulling me from my spiraling thoughts as he nudges my shoulder with his own. "It's okay."

I look up at him, at his beautiful blue eyes, and he smiles. I'm completely unnerved.

"You're awfully cool about this."

"What's the point in getting upset over an honest mistake?"

"Because I'm the reason we now have more mind numbing work ahead of us tonight."

"Eh, who has plans on a Thursday anyways?" And his smile is so charming it is unnerving. Maybe that's his plan, soften me up, I drop my guard and then WHAM he texts Judy about how I fucked up. Although, maybe he wouldn't. He doesn't seem to want the Fosters job at the end of the summer so maybe he really doesn't care that I just basically doubled our workload.

Because his plan was the only one offered, we get to work and less than an hour later we're back in our binding routine. I'm bringing a freshly bound report over to the table where Kyle is sitting assembling and my stomach growls. Loud. Like a feral beast who is reminding the creatures of surrounding wood that it's hungry. I cringe and hope against hope that Kyle didn't hear it.

No such luck.

"Someone's hungry huh," he says with a smirk on his face.

"Nah, just the ferocious animal who lives in my abdomen expressing its dissatisfaction at the lack of sustenance I've provided in the last six hours. He gets angry when he's only had coffee since lunch."

"Think he could get out and ruin the work we've done so far? Like if he's angry enough?"

Kyle's straight delivery, slightly worried, makes me smile.

"You can never be too sure."

"Well in that case let's go get food."

I grab my bag from the conference room and we walk down the hall to the elevator. He presses the call button and turns to me with his hands in his pockets. He isn't wearing his suit coat right now so I'm blessed with the no-tie-top-two-buttons-open-on-his-dress-shirt-sleeves-rolled-up-to-expose-delicious-forearms look.

Yeah, you could say I'm hungry.

Hungry for some man—

"What do you want for dinner?"

Pulled from my thoughts and feeling like I have drool dripping down my chin. I reply as Kyle holds the elevator door open for me. "Oh man, umm, I dunno."

"Well what do you feel like?"

Why does such a straightforward question have me in a panic? I'm so hungry that I could eat almost anything. Maybe he'll have something in mind.

"Whatever works for me."

He chuckles as the elevator descends.

"I'm not sure I've had 'whatever' before."

I give him a chastising look and then decide to just rattle it all off out loud because if he's not going to pick then he can help me sort through the laundry list of cuisines and food types rolling through my brain. We're both facing forward in the elevator like civilized people so I at least don't have to see his face when my particular brand of coo coo clock is on full display.

"Well, we could do Italian, Indian, BBQ, Thai, Pub Food, Sushi. Or like those sushi bowl things. Or sushi burritos. Ooo, tacos. And like I don't know if pizza sounds good but for some reason I could go for a calzone right now. Or like, a deli sandwich and potato chips."

The elevator opens to the lobby and I chance a glance at him and he's looking down at me smiling.

"Follow me," he says and steps out of the elevator.

He doesn't seem phased by my rambling off a dozen different food options. He seems almost amused by it. He's moving quickly and I have to take an extra little skip step to catch up to him at the revolving door. He starts to cross the street towards the bodega which is next to the deli we go to almost every day for lunch. I tag along but don't always get food. I don't have unlimited funds for lunches so I usually steal protein bars from the break room and eat one for lunch and take one home for dinner. Hey, it's not healthy, or doctor recommended, but I'm technically feeding myself and that's the best it's going to be right now.

Actually, I probably should have just grabbed a bar instead of leading Kyle on a wild goose chase for dinner. I'll get a drink at the bodega and call it a day. He can grab food and we'll head back.

We step into the bodega, Kyle hands me a basket and clears his throat.

"Liz, allow me to introduce you to a traditional Sutherland Snackooterie."

I laugh. "A *what?*"

"Sutherland Snackooterie. The dish that made me famous in college. The one my mom has been serving up every Friday night since I was a kid."

"Go on."

"First, we fill this basket with anything you want to eat."

"Anything?"

"Yes, anything. There isn't a set structure to a Snackooterie spread. Once we have this basket filled with chips, fruits, cookies, nuts, cheeses, crackers, we will buy it, take it back to the break room, and pour them onto a plate. Platter if available."

"Okay, I actually think this sounds fantastic."

"You actually think?" He says with a smirk. It's cute.

"Shut up. Yes. I think this sounds good."

"You said fantastic."

"Fine, yes, fantastic." And the eyeroll I throw at him doesn't hold any weight because my grin is a mile wide.

As we walk down the aisles he holds up different items and I get to decide if it's a yes or a no. We end up with sour cream and onion potato chips, ginger snap cookies, string cheese, almonds and chocolate covered raisins. We debated getting a six pack but ultimately decided that Fosters wouldn't appreciate us drinking on the job.

"It would be fun to go out for a drink though," I say as I pass by him through the door. He kind of stops short before following me out to the street.

"Ugh, yeah, that would be fun. Actually my buddies are meeting up tomorrow at a place in Brooklyn, Coopers. Would you want to come?"

"After the Fosters party?"

"Yeah, why not?"

Yeah, why not.

CHAPTER 5

LIZ

Leave it to Fosters, Henderson and Associates to rent out the Ritz Carlton ballroom for this 'casual drinks thing'. I have never seen a hotel this fancy. The ballroom has creamy wallpaper with a repeating floral pattern between framed out portions of the wall. The high top tables all have off white table clothes and somehow the small floral arrangements match the wallpaper exactly. It's like they pulled one right off the wall in some gimmick magic trick. The room has been arranged to promote mingling with a buffet table in the middle and two bars on the outside. Small upholstered benches sit under the tall windows along the back wall.

It is chic and sophisticated.

And my outfit is not up to par.

We had time to head home after work before this event. I made the mistake of sitting down and scrolling through social media looking for outfit inspiration only to surface an hour later and realize I was running late. In a mad dash I spruced up my makeup and changed clothes. I figured I'd have to dress up a little bit for the Fosters party. Pretty Business Casual. If that's a thing. But then I'm going straight to the Kyle & Friends drinks thing and it would be weird to pack a full outfit change.

I ended up in a pencil skirt with a v-neck t-shirt and a blazer. The t-shirt is definitely too casual. This crowd can spot 2-year-old cotton slub a mile away. And now I'm worried that with my pencil skirt I'll stick out like a sore thumb at Kyle's thing.

Maybe there's a busy store on the way to Brooklyn and I can shoplift a cute dress. Desperate times and all.

Distracted by sartorial stress and focused on the buffet table I'm walking towards, I don't notice Marcus Linard, Fosters, Henderson & Associates MedSci Division Partner, taking a parallel path to mine until he's standing at the table next to me and handing me a plate.

Let's stop for a minute to discuss Marcus Linard. Office dreamboat, non-profit sector sweetheart and I imagine, former college lacrosse player judging by his build and general demeanor. Tonight he is dressed in a gray suit that is tailored to perfection. His coat is unbuttoned and as he hands me the plate I can see the way his biceps flex with the movement. Through his jacket ladies. Tall, dark brown eyes, olive skin, and teeth so white you'd think they were color corrected. His haircut probably cost more than my outfit. I don't know if he's descended from greek gods but I wouldn't be surprised to learn it.

Not only is he attractive he is the top performing partner at Fosters. He brings in more clients than anyone else. So he's a hottie with a body who also spends his days helping others. If he tells me a story about volunteering for cancer kids I might melt into a puddle on the spot.

I reach for a deconstructed something or other on a chip and try to take a demure bite when the whole thing crumbles into my palm and down my chin. I let out a half giggle, half croak noise like a troll who got a night off from bridge duty, and hear Marcus scoff softly.

"Best to just put it all in your mouth at once." He says with a sly smile.

I almost choke.

He laughs and then offers me a napkin. As I wipe my chin he slides vegetables and hummus onto his plate.

Fuck me, he's a healthy eater too.

"How has your first week at Fosters been Liz?"

OMIGAWD he knows my name.

I'm sweating.

"Oh, well you know, amazing and grueling and I can't believe how much I've learned already. Sure it's been mostly waiting for faxes and then sending different faxes after waiting for updates from consultants. Oh and binding reports. I hear the binding machine in my sleep already."

He takes the moment I pause for a breath as an opening, thank his Greek god ancestors. "I remember my internship and I don't know that I'd call it amazing but grueling sounds about right. Sort of trial by fire. Drinking from a firehose and all that. Who's project are you assigned to now?"

"I just wrapped up deliverables for Mercy Hospital."

"Ah that's my project!"

"I thought it was Donald presenting."

"Don and I handle the account together. I fly out Monday. Too bad I didn't know sooner or I would have included you more in the process."

My mouth goes dry. I need something to drink. And hold on to. His eye contact is making my knees shake.

"Thank you," I manage to squeak out. "I want to be successful here. I'd love to work more closely with you."

"I'd like that. I can tell already that you're dedicated. I'll make sure you're assigned to my next project too. Enjoy the rest of your night."

With that he winks at me.

Winks.

Then he turns and walks away.

"Oh, okay, yeah, thanks, you too." I mumble to his retreating back. And I look around the room for the bar.

G&T in hand I find my fellow interns in the corner by the windows. Nora catches my eye contact first and kind of wiggles her eyebrows.

"AWW yeah Liz!" She whisper shouts while doing a hip roll thing that might be considered a dance move if we weren't at a stuffy, sophisticated work event around clients. "Marcus Linard was just flirting with you SO HARD! How did you keep yourself standing up straight?"

"Ha, urm, what do you mean? I don't think he was flirting, just being friendly. He was just talking about the Mercy presentation on Monday." Did she see the wink though?

"I don't understand what girls see in him," Chandler says half to his beer bottle.

"You don't have to worry about what we see in him... we just see it." Nora replies while giving Chandler a friendly punch on the arm. "And I just saw Marc The Shark totally circling Liz's chum."

Kyle barely catches his spit take response. Then coughs to recover. Nora pats him on the back.

"You okay there pal?" She teases.

Kyle just clears his throat and takes another sip. He has kept his gaze on me the whole time. I square my shoulders in his direction, hopefully signaling an end to the Marc The Shark conversation, and ask "So, where is this bar we're going to tonight?"

Nora and Chandler, and Kyle for that matter, look at me shocked. And I realize, too late, that I was the only one invited.

"Oh, shit, no I meant. Ummm, isn't everyone going?"

The look on Nora's face confirms it. I was the only intern invited to Kyle's group hang later.

Kyle's hand is forced and he shares the details with the others. His buddy Jeff lives just down the street from this place and it's where they've been hanging out most Friday nights since they all moved to the city.

I'll be way over dressed for that.

CHAPTER 6

KYLE

Small talk is unbearable. Small talk with people you're meant to impress is even worse. Marcus and Lauren had Liz and I talk to several different clients at the Fosters party. I was glad to have time getting to know Liz better but I didn't really care what any of the clients had to say. Liz is funny and confident and I admire how easily she can talk to new people. I spent most of the event standing next to her and just staring. She has an effortless sense of humor that endears people to her, myself included. I can't seem to get enough.

Marcus shakes hands with the client we were talking to and then turns towards us. He takes Liz by the elbow and walks us towards an older woman in a pink skirt suit.

"I'm going to introduce you to Agatha Sanderson, the widow of Sanderson Labs founder William Sanderson. Now even though Bill founded it and has passed away Agatha is still very much involved and works to bring in a lot of donations from her network."

He stands up tall and clears his throat.

"Mrs. Sanderson, so good to see you again."

"Aah Marc my boy, don't you look handsome tonight. Thank you for inviting me, James always puts on the best soirees." Her tone is formal but also somehow playful. I get the feeling this lady gets what she wants every time she asks.

"He does. Mrs. Sanderson—"

"It's Agatha darling."

"Of course, Agatha, allow me to introduce the two summer interns who will be working on the Sanderson Labs project this summer. This is Liz Collins and Kyle Sutherland. Both are bright young people who have come to Fosters from Ivy League institutions."

"Ah yes, nothing but the best for Fosters & Associates." Agatha concedes. "Now, youngsters, what are you two up to tonight?"

I feel Liz look up at me.

I felt bad when she slipped up about Cooper's tonight with Nora and Chandler. She looked embarrassed. I had gotten the impression that Chandler had a variety of options he could choose from on a Friday night and that Nora would want to go home and relax. She's super focused at the office and I just didn't get the 'chill at a bar' vibe from her. We'll see.

"Actually, some friends of mine are meeting at a bar in Brooklyn so we will be headed there later." I tell Agatha. I had to stop myself from saying 'ma'am' I didn't think she'd appreciate it.

"Marcus, why are you making these fine young people stand around here and talk to me? Let them get on with their night!"

Marcus laughs and opens his mouth but Agatha cuts him off.

"And you deary," she leans in to whisper to Liz, who leans in a little too, "do whatever you can to keep this charming young man! You're such an adorable couple and will make very attractive babies. Not yet of course, at this point just give him enough so he doesn't go anywhere else."

Agatha leans in further and whispers something that sounds a lot like. "A good blowie every now and then should do the job until he proposes."

Liz's eyes double in size as she listens to this old lady talk about blow jobs. My dick curls up into itself hearing the same thing.

Then I picture Liz giving me a *blowie* and my cock almost jumps for joy.

Settle down man.

"Agatha," Marcus scolds, "These two are just peers at work. But you're right, they are young and deserve to enjoy themselves. I'm glad you came tonight and we'll be in touch soon."

Marcus reaches out to shake her hand.

I do the same.

Liz follows and Agatha pulls her in close and whispers something in her ear that I can't hear but I can see Liz blush.

Her skin turns peachy with embarrassment and her big round eyes dance from side to side.

I would love to know what advice she received.

I would love to know what she's thinking about being linked with me.

I wouldn't mind being linked with her.

Liz and I walk over to where Nora and Chandler are still standing by the window.

"Marcus's client just told us to go out and be young." Liz shares while taking a sip of her G&T from the straw. Her cheeks cave in and lust shoots through me.

"Among other things." I mumble.

Liz gives me a look that screams *don't say anything* so I leave it at that.

Nora tilts her head back and downs the rest of her drink. "Alright, bitches, let's roll." I mentally move Nora to the 'work hard, play hard' category.

Now that we're all in a cab together I'm actually feeling nervous about them meeting my friends. I've known Jeff since freshman year of college. We were both management and finance majors, we both didn't want anything to do with Greek life on campus, both like golf, both got grad degrees right away, and we even studied abroad in London together.

Liz is sitting between Nora and Chandler in the back seat and the girls are singing along to the song on the radio. Liz has her feet propped up on the center console and I unintentionally peek down her skirt when I turn around.

I still can't believe it's the same girl from interview day. But when she crashed into me in the lobby on Monday I knew it instantly. When she made the mistake on the cover sheet I saw her entire demeanor dim and it gutted me. Was I annoyed? Of course, but getting upset about it wouldn't help anyone.

I loved being able to share a Snackooterie with her too. I haven't had one since I was home right after graduation and while that's only been a few weeks it feels longer. That late night working with her has been the highlight of interning at Fosters so far.

Because the actual work itself is painfully boring. Thank goodness Liz wants to make the work more exciting. She is obviously bored out of her mind with the paperwork we're doing but she makes it fun anyways.

Once we had the incorrect reports re-done, she set a timer and we raced to see who could bind a report faster.

I smile as I recall the memory. I've been staring at her face and suddenly she lifts her gaze and makes eye contact with me.

We both blush.

She caught me thinking about her.

Maybe I caught her thinking about me?

I am crushing. Hard.

I pivot and stare straight out the windshield for the remainder of the ride.

"Heeeeeeeey!" my friends call when they see us walk in. I'm smiling but it's forced. Even though work this week was brainless, I'm exhausted. I also know that my friends are lying in wait to embarrass me in front of the Fosters interns so I'm gearing myself up to be a good sport.

From behind the group, Tiffany appears and makes her way over quickly. She launches into my arms, gives me a huge hug, plants a kiss on my lips, and links her arm through mine to escort me over to the table. She laughs at my shocked face because she knows she didn't tell me she was back. She went home to Ft. Lauderdale after graduation with the promise to be in the city after a week with some friends from high school but that week stretched into four.

So the cat's out of the bag. I've kinda got a girlfriend.

Tiff and I met last fall. She loves being the center of attention and I think she likes that I don't. We hooked up after a night out and we've kind of been doing that ever since.

In the last month we haven't talked much at all. I was moving and starting my internship. She was partying and sleeping in. It's telling that she and I didn't try to stay close while she was away. We're more like friends with benefits. Well, even that's too much of a relationship. We're people who hang in the same circle of friends and hook up at the end of the night.

Yeah, that's it.

"Guys, meet Tiffany..." The end of the sentence just hangs there. I will *not* call her my girlfriend but you don't actually introduce someone as your fuck buddy and my same-circle-of-friends-and-we-hook-up label doesn't roll off the tongue easily.

"Hi Tiffany, I'm Nora. This is Liz and Chandler. We work with Kyle. Now, tell me all his embarrassing stories!"

Tiffany laughs, grabs Nora by the arm, and drags her to the bar. I can't even begin to imagine what stories she's telling. Chandler is standing at our table but staring off at a table of girls across the bar. Liz is looking at me with her sparkling eyes but I catch a hint of confusion.

Does she think Tiffany is my girlfriend? I mean the big kiss might do it.

Has Liz picked up that I am into her?

I mean not that I'm *into* into her. It's too soon for that.

I will say I'm surprised by how vibrant and fun she is and how she's unlike any other girl I've ever met and I've only known her for a few days.

Tiffany and Nora come back to the table and Tiff must see the look Liz is giving me. It's not quite flirty but there is interest there. I hope.

Before I can try to figure out the feelings that have rushed through me in the last two minutes Tiffany grabs me by the scruff of my neck and plants a long kiss on me right there in the middle of the bar.

Liz's eyes are wide and my cheeks are burning when Tiffany pulls back. What the hell?

"Ew! Get a room!" Jeff yells from the bar before walking over to us "No one wants to see Kyle kiss anyone right?" he says to Liz as he steps next to her. "Hi, I'm Jeff, what can I get you to drink?"

"Vodka, for my eyeballs, and a Gin and Tonic for my brain." Liz says with a laugh.

"G&T gal huh? That's very sophisticated of you." Jeff gives her the 'after you' arm towards the bar. I see him get a look at her ass in the skirt and I feel my shoulders tense.

CHAPTER 7

LIZ

Okay, the shots were a bad idea. Kyle's friends are super fun and Jeff is really cute. I've learned that he has a vespa scooter to get around town on, that he's starting as a first year at a law firm where his uncle is a partner and that his dad is a real estate developer who owns apartment buildings around Brooklyn. That's how he has such a, and I quote, "sick place."

Nora left a while ago, Chandler is chatting up a girl who came in with her friends earlier. Kyle is talking with Tiffany who keeps putting her hands on his thigh or curling her fingers through the scruff at the back of his neck. I don't think I've seen her take her hands off him.

I myself am at a high top table alone with Jeff.

Not that I wanted to hang out with Kyle but I expected we would hang out a little more than we have tonight. But now that I think about it I can barely look at him after what Agatha whispered to me. It was embarrassing enough having her suggest I keep him interested with often enough *blowies* but her suggestion to have him catch me playing with my nipples was too much to handle.

And my nipples totally popped when she whispered it in my ear.

I know myself, I will now and forever more think of giving Kyle blowies and playing with my nipples in front of him because this filthy old woman suggested it. I mean, I'm picturing it now and I watch Tiffany slide her hand up his bicep and give a little squeeze.

"Hey, you wanna get out of here? My place is around the corner."

I return my attention to Jeff quickly before I burst out laughing. His face looks so crestfallen I laugh a little more before grabbing his arm and saying "Oh, no I'm laughing because that's a terrible line! And probably a red flag for most girls. Luckily for you, I'm not most girls and I really want to flop on a sofa with snacks right now."

"I can make that happen." Jeff says with a smile. "Are you a late night pizza, fries, or burrito girl?"

"Yes."

He smiles. "I know a place, c'mon."

Jeff starts walking me towards the water and after two blocks we round a corner and the most beautiful sight these drunk eyes have ever seen is before me. An entire city block of food trucks all lined up in a row. On both sides. I cannot contain myself and I squeal with delight.

"Wanna do a lap and see all the options?" Jeff asks me.

"Great idea."

I think I am actually drooling as we walk past a series of colorful trucks offering pizza by the slice, tacos, BBQ, burgers, donuts, grilled cheese and loaded fries. While my mouth is drooling, my eyes are fixated on the repeating patterns the trucks make. How one has stripes and the next is solid and next to each other they make a compelling visual. I catch the details of the people waiting in line to order. Chipped toenail polish among a circle of girls teetering on heeled sandals as they talk about their night out. Couples leaning on each other. Dudes shoveling half of their pizza slices into their mouths at once.

"What looks good?" Jeff asks, breaking my fixation on the way empty containers have been stacked haphazardly against the already full trash can.

"Everything! This place is a dream come true. Let's start with pizza."

Pizza slices in hand - veggie for me, supreme for Jeff - we walk over to a spot on the curb with a view of the water. Jeff offers to go and get us lemonades and by the time he is walking back I've taken down half of the pizza slice.

"Did they only give you half?" He asks jokingly.

I smile, "Ugh, no. I'm just so freaking hungry. The food at the Fosters thing was like finger foods. Not enough. Nothing like a proper *Snackooterie*."

"Kyle introduced you to *Snackooterie* already?! It took him a full year to share it with me." I look at him as surprised as I can with a piece of veggie pizza hanging from my lips. He laughs. "It's the best, right?"

"The pizza or *Snackooterie*?" I ask with a mouthful.

"Both I guess."

"Yeah, both are the best." I wash the last of my slice down with the lemonade.

"Wanna finish the rest upstairs?" Jeff nods towards the building behind him.

"Yes, and I'm grabbing one of those walking tacos and curly fries on the way up." I grin.

Jeff's place is nice. Like grown up nice. The timber loft building is a historic landmark. Jeff's dad's company buys old buildings and restores them as either offices or condos or both. Jeff plans to eventually work with his dad but in the legal department. He's seen too many deals go sideways from poor legal coverage. Not exactly a public defender but still a protector who is driven by helping others. I can get on board with that kind of purpose in a boyfriend.

After we enjoy the fries and walking tacos, which might be my new favorite food consisting of taco fixings piled on top of frito chips in the chip bag, we start a movie.

It's been a minute since I've gone home with a guy and about ten minutes into the movie I realize that he's probably thinking there will be some action tonight. I'm not opposed to the idea. Not super into it either. There is a thing as being too tired right?

It's not that I'm thinking about his friend.

Jeff has been looking over my direction every once in a while and this time when he does I keep my gaze forward but smile wide.

"What?" He asks.

"Just thinking it'd be fun to make out for a bit." I say with a shrug. The picture of nonchalance.

"I think that would be fun." Jeff says as he scootches closer to me on the sofa.

Maybe it's the booze. Maybe it's the exhaustion. Maybe it's the walking taco (and pizza and fries) but this makeout session isn't great. It's a little sloppy but not in an intense way. Like his kisses are too big, the inside of his lips are like around mine or something. I know trying to figure out why the makeout is weird isn't helping me get past the fact that it's weird but this series of kisses is doing nothing for me.

Zip.

Zilch.

Nada.

No flutter of my heart. No heat flushing my cheeks. No throbbing of my lady parts.

When Jeff pulls back. I am terrified that he's going to ask me if everything is okay and I'm going to have to lie to him to protect his feelings and then he'll dive right back in for more.

"You're super cute Liz," Jeff starts. And, glory be, I can hear the *but* coming. "But" *yes there it is,* "I'm not sure we're the best make out buddies."

I laugh because, phew, he wasn't feeling it ethier.

"I agree. That was more weird than good."

He scrunches his face up and I realize I sound like I just called his kissing weird. Which, it was, but I'm a nicer person than that.

"No, I mean, it was, umm, nice. But like, yeah, what you said, we're not the best make out buddies."

He smiles, thankfully, and looks towards his bedroom.

Oh no. I'm not gonna do *that* with him after a weird make out.

"It's late. Do you want me to get you an Uber home or do you want to just stay over? You can have the bed and I'll sleep out here."

I smile because, seriously, what a nice guy.

"I'll stay if that's okay. I'm feeling really sleepy." Plus his apartment is so much nicer than mine.

"Of course, c'mon, I'll get you all set up."

CHAPTER 8

KYLE

I'm the first intern in the office on Monday. Being early is a trait I inherited from my mom who is always early. I turn on the lights in our conference room and check the chat for anything the consultants might need at the last minute for the Mercy presentation today.

Nora saunters in next, nodding a less-than-enthusiastic good morning. Her client, Stanford University, is coming into the office today. Usually Fosters goes to the client, on their dime, but the President and Provost are in New York for a conference. The Development team came too and there is a meeting here at Fosters and lunches and dinners with big east coast donors. Nora is tasked with prospect research and preparing the team for the lunches and dinners with the donors. I don't think she has to create a binder with their faces and details but she does have to prep them with interests and connections so the Fosters team can have intelligent conversations with the prospects.

Chandler and Liz were on the same elevator up. She smiles at me when she enters the room and I offer her a half smile back. I realize that the last time I saw her she had Jeff's hand on the small of her back and I am just now realizing how much that has nagged at me all weekend.

"How was the weekend? Did you and Tiffany have fun?" she asks as she sits down next to me and pulls up the Mercy presentation on her laptop.

"Yeah, a lot of mimosas that had to be posted to Insta before I could drink them but it was good to see her. How was yours?"

"Good! I mean, yeah, it was fine." she leans closer to me and whispers "Wait is this weird? I hung out with Jeff all weekend."

"Nope."

Yep.

Definitely weird.

She smiles. "My roommate had a friend in town too so it worked out. Although I had to fumigate my suit for today because I think she used the apartment as a hot box all weekend."

"When are you going to invite us over to get high Liz?" Chandler chimes in.

"Ha, I'm not. My roommate isn't the fun times pothead, she's the totally zombied out pothead. It's a lot of Dave Matthews live albums and patchouli."

"You gotta get out of there Liz. Like you're so serious about getting this Fosters job you can't walk in here every day reeking like that!" Nora is showing some of her inner Goody Two Shoes.

"Yeah I know Nora. It was the only place I could afford. It's only a few more weeks until I either have a salary or I move back home. I'll spend what little disposable income I have on Febreeze."

"Ooor" Nora stretches the word into five syllables, "go shack up with Jeff! You did it all weekend anyways."

"Did not!" Liz sputters and tosses a pen cap at Nora.

"Did too!"

"Did not!"

"Did t-*ahem*" Nora covers her response with a cough as Judy walks in to tell us what tortures await this week.

CHAPTER 9

LIZ

While I could have killed Nora for suggesting I move in with Jeff I'd be lying if I said I didn't have fun this weekend. After staying at his place Friday night we grabbed iced coffee and bagels and he walked me back to my apartment. It was a beautiful day and we chatted easily. He offered up a lot of information about his family and his friend group. He, oddly, talked a lot about Tiffany. I couldn't decide if he was telling me all about her because I knew Kyle or if he was telling me all about her because he thought she and I could be friends or if he was talking all about her because he likes her.

Honestly, I think it's that he *likes her*, likes her.

I can't put my finger on it but I can read people and he kinda had *crushin'* written all over his face.

Luckily for me Jeff is a wealth of New York City knowledge so I asked him all my questions. He knows where the best bodegas, bagels, and babkas are. Unluckily those three bests are at like opposite sides of the island. He took me to the babka spot which was on the way back to Brooklyn so I grabbed a cinnamon and we parted ways.

I might not have made a love connection but I do have a new friend in the city and that is no small feat.

Kyle kind of clammed up when Nora gave me shit about staying with Jeff. I didn't get a chance to clarify that it was just one night, and that nothing besides a weird mini make out happened. Now I'm wondering why I feel like I need to explain that to Nora. To Kyle.

Hmm.

It is so typical for me to crush on an unavailable guy. Or unattainable since most of my intense crushes up until this point have been of the celebrity variety.

It's almost 5pm and I'm refreshing my email hoping to hear how the Mercy presentation went. Instead the phone in the center of the conference table rings. I answer it on speakerphone.

"Fosters, Henderson and Associates, this is Liz, how can I help you?"

"Liz! Hi! It's Marcus and Don." Marcus says from his side of the phone.

"Hello! How did the meeting go today?" Kyle walks in and I point to the phone and mouth 'Marcus' so he comes closer and stands right next to me. Casually he places both his hands on the table and props himself up to listen in. His fingers are spread wide. Palms flat. They're big, manly. And for the first time ever I'm attracted to the veins in a man's hand.

And, oh my, he smells good. Like an outdoor shower. Woodsy and fresh.

"The meeting went really well." Marcus says seriously then off to the side he says "Okay, Don, thanks, I'll talk to you later. Liz, you still there?"

"Yes, I'm here." I don't know why I don't say that Kyle is here too.

"Good. The presentation was amazing. You did a killer job with it. And the client was excited about the projections we presented. Now the real work begins and I can't wait to work with you back in the office."

I blush and I can also feel Kyle's gaze on me. I'm a little flabbergasted and I don't know what to say so the best I can muster is a timid "Sounds good Marcus."

"It sounds more than good! Maybe we need to get you out on the road so you can experience these meetings with me."

He's just being a mentor. Not hitting on me.

"I've never been to Texas so it would be a lot of fun to attend a meeting at Mercy." Kyle stands up with a little push at the table and walks out of the room. I watch him go.

"Consider it done then Liz. Thank you again. I couldn't have done it without your help on the backend."

"Sure thing Marcus, Kyle and I put a lot of effort into the report." Sorry that Kyle didn't hear me say that.

"Yes, well, Kyle is great and all but I'd much rather have your company in client meetings than his." And I'm not sorry that Kyle didn't hear that.

I hang up with Marcus after fielding a few more awkward but nice comments and sit back in my chair. My phone pings with a text.

JEFF: Hey - wanna grab dinner tonight?

ME: Sure! When? Where?

JEFF: I'll pick you up at the office. Tell Kyle, he and Tiffany are coming too.

I blink. Umm, sure I guess. Is this a double date? Jeff and I are *not* suited for a romantic relationship.

I spin and kick Kyle's chair as he's moving to sit in it so it slides a little. He gives me this one eyebrow look that says 'you tryin' to mess with me?' and I grin because maybe there is a fun loving side to him after all "Yo. I've been told to tell you that you're coming to dinner tonight with me and Jeff and Tiffany."

"Oh. Ok. Cool." He deadpans.

Or maybe there is no fun loving side of him because that was the most unenthusiastic response to an impromptu Monday night double date, but also not a date, ever.

CHAPTER 10

KYLE

"I wonder if getting a Fosters tattoo will help me get the job?" Liz says out of nowhere while we're waiting together for Jeff and Tiffany. I've never been great at starting social conversations. This is a skill I'm going to need to learn to some degree or the next forty years of my work life are going to be rough.

I can't help but laugh at Liz's comment though. "Nah, I think they'd file that under a dress code violation or something."

"True. Dang. Well now I'll just have to work harder than you and hope I get it. No offense."

"None taken. I'm not gunning for it."

"Oh yeah, that's right. Your Aunt with YouthFull! That's seriously such an amazing connection. I'm jealous. So with a job already lined up, why are you working here as a fundraising slave?"

I chuckle. "Aunt Mary is my hero. She said I couldn't come and work for her right out of school because she didn't have the time to teach me everything. So, I'm here at Fosters trying to learn as much as I can before going to work with her."

Tiffany and Jeff stroll up and we all decide to try an Italian Bistro a few blocks down.

At dinner I notice how much Liz and Jeff are flirting. And how much I'm paying attention to the two of them instead of Tiffany. Luckily she's none the wiser and is completely absorbed in telling us about the list of parties her PR firm will be in charge of this fall.

Jeff seems to know the parties and has been to a few himself. I knew his family was a part of the New York social scene, I just never paid attention to how connected they really were. Liz seems to be just nodding along and isn't adding anything to the conversation. This is the quietest I've seen her in the time I've known her.

"I think I'm most excited for the art gallery parties." Tiffany says as she takes a bite of her pasta.

"I'd buy art if I had the income for it. I could spend all day looking at pieces. All styles too. The Guggenheim is like my favorite place on earth." Liz says with a glimmer in her eye I haven't seen before.

"The Guggenheim?" Tiffany swallows hard. "Don't you mean The Louvre? I'd even settle for The Met," she finishes with a scoff.

I watch Liz bristle and then lean in with her elbows on the table before defending her choice. "Well, I haven't been to the Louvre but The Met is too stuffy for my taste. Art is about feelings and conveying emotion and I connect more with the pieces at the Guggenheim."

"I haven't been to any of these." I add trying to break the cycle of Tiffany wanting to one-up Liz. "I'm excited to see more music at different venues here in the city. We went to such dingy ones in school."

"Ha I know. Some of those were real dives." Jeff provides while slinging his arm over the back of Liz's chair. I feel my own body tense up at the sight.

Tiffany says "Gross." while Liz says "Fun!" in unison and I smile at Liz. She catches it and looks down at her lap while smiling at herself as she readjusts her napkin.

"Since buying concert tickets will probably be out of my budget for a while I'd love to find some free shows to catch this summer. Is there a concert in the park series or anything like that?"

"Well, actually, I know where you can catch some free music." Jeff says leaning closer to Liz while looking at me. I shake my head no and he nods that he understands. Liz passes a look back and forth between us before focusing on Jeff who continues, "That bar we went to Friday, Coopers, has live music most Saturday nights."

"That's so fun! I'll have to come and check it out sometime."

"Yeah, that would be so fun," Tiffany says but her tone isn't sincere. It's like she's agreeing to give a toddler a rocket ship for Christmas knowing full well it isn't going to happen. "Why don't we meet there on Saturday?"

"I totally would but Chandler invited us out to the Hamptons this weekend and I'm going to take advantage of that while I can." Liz says while looking at me.

"Yeah, I meant to ask you about that Tiff, would you want to go?" I ask.

"Seriously? Yes, I would but I've got my first event on Friday and then a brunch on Saturday so it isn't going to work."

"Do I get an invite?" Jeff asks Liz.

"I can definitely ask," she replies with a genuine smile that lights up her eyes even in the shade of this street corner patio. If Liz is interested in Jeff I'll do everything I can not to spoil it for her. For them. But feeling how my body reacts to her presence and bristles at her connection with Jeff I know one thing.

I need to end whatever it is going on between Tiffany and me.

"So are you in?" Chandler asks as he sets down a stack of binders.

"For what?" I ask since I've been elbow deep in reconciling donor data from one database to another all morning.

"The Hamptons man! I've gotta tell the staff how many rooms to get ready. Nora and Liz are in but aren't bringing anyone so they'll share one of the bunk rooms. Are you bringing your girlfriend?"

"Oh, ugh," Liz isn't bringing Jeff. Is there a reason? Was Jeff busy? He did walk her home last night but he texted me about the Mets game late so I don't think he stayed over. Should I just ask Jeff? I could ask Liz, she's just down the hall in the breakroom. But that feels so middle school.

Do you like me?

Check yes or no.

But that's what this is right? I like Liz. I'm drawn to her. And even though I told Tiffany last night that I thought she was rude to Liz I didn't actually break up with her. It was difficult to manage once she came back with me and immediately initiated a makeout session.

And I was thinking about it, I'm honestly not sure we need to officially break up. Like it has been a series of hook ups over a few, okay 9 months time. We have a classic situationship on our hands here. Some shared experiences but not a full relationship. I never bought her flowers or really thought of her unless we were together.

My phone pings, I realize I haven't replied to Chandler yet but I look at it anyways.

TIFFANY: Hey babe, sorry I was rude to Liz last night. I'm nervous about the job starting.

TIFFANY: Nervous and excited. But I'm also excited to come home to you after the party on Friday and tell you all about it. It feels so good to have you in my corner! You're the best. XO!

Now I'm officially confused.

Yeah I'm attracted to Liz and we connect on an emotional level but I feel like maybe I owe it to Tiffany to give a relationship a shot. Give her some time to settle into the new job. We are becoming closer friends with benefits I guess. It will be nice to see her this weekend and be there for her. And, I'm attracted to Tiffany too, let's be honest, she's hot.

Okay, I've got my answer for the Hamptons.

"Nah man, I wish I could. Next time for sure."

CHAPTER 11

LIZ

Is taking the bus really how people get to the Hamptons? I kind of figured it would at least be a string of town cars. But alas, those of us looking to get out of the city for 36 hours will gladly cram onto a bus. When I got the Fosters offer I did not expect that a weekend in the Hamptons would come my way. I'm not sure what I expected to be doing on the weekends but it was probably sitting in the apartment reading a book too overwhelmed by the idea that I'd get lost trying to find something.

At least Chandler is with me tonight. I'm honestly afraid that I'd get on the wrong bus or miss my stop or somehow manage to do both. Weirder things have happened.

I have learned to navigate the city by foot and as a passenger in a cab but public transportation eludes me. I only take the train to the office. A few weeks ago I tried to take the bus to the west side to find one of the spots Jeff had recommended and ended up in the financial district.

I decided to just walk home.

Nora is taking the next bus out because she had a call later in the day with Stanford. She was oddly excited to sit silently and listen in. Lauren and Marcus don't give us a lot of opportunity to talk with the clients so Kyle and I have just been spending our days doing data comparisons. Today I got to proofread a proposal that is 90% boilerplate and 10% custom but some of the templates they pull together are in a different font or size or even color so I'm checking for formatting as well. It was painfully boring. Frustrating.

Chandler and I board the bus, he gives me the window seat and I rest my head against the glass as I slump down and sigh. It was a long week.

"Whoa! Penny for your thoughts?" Chandler asks while elbowing me in the side.

"I'm exhausted. I think I proofread a 30,000 word document today about data and analysis and stats and findings and blah blah blah blah blah blah blah." I say while rolling my eyes.

"That's what you were doing? Woof."

"Oh it gets better. Because I can't keep track of all those words I decided to, ya know, double my work and create graphs and charts and other visual aids to help me keep everything straight. No one will ever see the visuals because they're so focused on doing it the way it's always been done but it helped me. I'm kinda waiting for the right client to use them on."

"Just going to sneak it in? That's bold. Foster doesn't really like, you know, surprises."

"I know. Maybe in a few years when I'm a lead on the client team. We'll see."

"Fair enough. But we aren't going to talk about work anymore. It's the weekend!" Chandler squeals.

"Ha, you're right. Okay, so since we're both working at the same terrible internship and my only hobby is reading romance novels, what do you want to talk about?"

"Cards." Chandler says while standing up to get something out of his backpack that he stored in the rack above our heads. "And, juice." He adds with a wink as he sits back down with a deck of cards and shakes a flask at me.

"THAT will make cards a lot more fun. Give it here." I reach for the flask, knock back a swig, and immediately regret it.

"UGH! What *is* that?"

"Coconut Rum." He replies as if I should already know that. "Reminds me of vacation."

"Okay, fine but warn a girl." I trade the flask for the deck of cards. "How about Gin Rummy?"

"Deal em."

The bus ride continued with much of the same and once I was used to the fact that coconut rum was coming my way when I took a drag from the flask I quickly came around to it and decided it reminds me of vacation too.

I learned about Chandler's rescue pup, Jesse, who he has had for six months now. Luckily his parents own the apartment he's in so not only does he have room for a dog it's technically okay with the building management. My apartment, by contrast, is so mismanaged and old that there are absolutely no animals allowed except for the mice that live in the basement with the laundry machines. I am fully aware that they could be rats but I am choosing to believe they are an adorable gang of helpful mouses like in Cinderella.

Whatever helps me sleep at night right?

Our bus comes to a stop and when I stand up I realize what several shots of coconut rum does to a girl on an empty stomach. I'm a little bit wobbly. I had intended to spend the weekend next to the pool reading and relaxing and checking out. But at this rate I might as well have a big night tonight and take it easy tomorrow.

Chandler carries my duffel towards a black Mercedes G-Class SUV and then suddenly the lights flash and it unlocks. I realize that it's his. I've *never* been in a luxury car like this. Sure in college a few of my friends had nice cars but they were hand-me-downs or they had to share them with siblings. Maybe it's the coconut rum talking but Chandler just got a little bit cuter.

At least through the one eye that can focus when I wink the other closed.

"So the car was just here waiting for you? How does that work?" I ask, my small town showing.

"Brando, the house manager, brings it to the station when we're headed out. You'll meet him soon. I had him stock up on those granola bars you're always grabbing from the break room too."

Well shit.

Embarrassment runs through my veins and I feel my shoulders curl in on themselves. I didn't think anyone noticed that I was stealing granola bars to eat at home. If Chandler noticed has Fosters noticed? Is that going to be an issue? Fuck. I didn't think that through.

But on the other hand that was really thoughtful of Chandler and he might have gotten even a little bit cuter just now. Let me check with my winky eye… yep. Cute.

Yes, "boyfriend" is on my Big Girl List but a guy like Chandler isn't the guy for me. I like a guy who has to work for it.

An underdog maybe?

Although, an alpha dog might not be bad.

Chandler isn't really any of those things since he comes from money, has his own apartment, and is just doing this job to fill his time slash to appease his parents. Plus he's cute but not really doing it for me. I think the best way to play this is as if we're old pals.

"Aww buddy, thanks! I'll have to steal some from your house too because those are my dinners most nights."

"Seriously? That's what you eat for dinner?"

"That or PB&J. Honestly I just get home most nights and hang out in my room to edit photos and stuff. My craigslist roommate smokes a lot of pot and I've found that just by hanging in my room she'll leave me alone."

"You don't want to join her?"

"Not every night. I did last Saturday for a bit but I got all antsy and ended up in my room making a list of photographs to take so I guess it helped me be productive but I didn't need the jitters."

"I hear ya. I used to smoke a lot in college but it got kinda old. Now it's mostly booze. I had Brando stock the fridges for us too. And Carolina will make whatever you want for your meals so please eat more than granola bars this weekend."

"That I can do."

We drive a few minutes and then pull into a gravel driveway that is lined with trees. Through them I can see a brown wood shingled house with white trim and a turquoise door. There are big blooming white hydrangea plants along the front and a little white picket fence with a gable gate at the end of the drive. The house looks smaller than I was expecting but it is beautifully charming.

The windows of the SUV are open and Chandler's "Miami Chill" playlist has been blaring as we drove over. It honestly feels a little dream like. Once we park and get out of the car I can hear more music and pool splashes and shrieks coming from behind the house.

"Sounds like Adam and his buddies are already here."

"Who is Adam?"

"My twin." Chandler looks at me like I just asked what 2 + 2 is.

"What? You never told us you had a twin!"

"Ha really? Shit. Well, yeah, I've got a twin, his name is Adam. Technically he's older. He's named after my dad but I'm my mom's favorite. He's here with a buddy or two and our cousin Fiona and her girlfriend are coming too."

"Oh wow, full house." I mutter while we walk through the gate to the back yard. After a few more steps I stop in my tracks because in front of me is the most beautiful backyard imaginable. A crystal clear pool glistens in the sun as two couples battle out a chicken fight, behind them are a line of white lounge chairs stacked high with cushions in the same aquamarine as the front door. Each unoccupied chair has a tan and white striped turkish towel rolled up like a lumbar pillow inviting me to lounge there for a luxurious amount of time. My eyes keep scanning to the right and land on a bar set up in the outdoor kitchen which is part of the back patio.

Which is off the rest of the house.

The charming little square I saw from the driveway is only the beginning. There is a-whole-nother wing off the back here. It's easily twice as much space as the front of the house. A covered walkway connects the patio to the rooms along the back section. All three sets of wide french doors bracketed by potted topiaries look to be similarly arranged so I'm guessing it's a string of bedrooms.

I'm taking in the perfectly manicured lawn and terracotta pots filled with white blooms of different types and the soft glow from the hanging bulb lights. My mind goes into a frenzy framing beautiful shots and setting up a garden party scene for lifestyle photos.

"Yo, earth to Liz!" Chandler calls out.

I turn towards him and smile and wave.

"This is Adam and his friend Jake. Here we have Fiona and her girlfriend Jen. Over there is Paul and Colin and Rico. Ugh, everyone, this is Liz."

I'm greeted with a chorus of Heys and Sups and waves. I sheepishly smile back and wave. Chandler makes his way over and leads the way across the patio, past the wrought iron dining set, and into the house. We step in through the back door and I can tell you now that I am as impressed with the interiors of this home as I am the exterior.

All the walls are a creamy white, not stark, but bright and homey. The high ceilings of this main living area are painted the same color with dark stained exposed beams running from the sides to the middle. There are a few sky lights in the gabled ceiling which make the room feel even brighter than it already is.

Two, white, oversized sofas face each other and they look well loved. Not in a run down sort of way, in an invitingly lumpy way. The coffee table has a few New York Photography books, a giant candle, and a chess board sitting on it. Along the shelves on the back wall are framed photographs of people at life's celebrations - graduations, birthdays, weddings - a collection of smiles and moments.

It is clear that Chandler's family love this home and use it whenever they can.

The kitchen cabinets are white, they've got that thing where the fridge is covered in a cabinet door. Pure sophistication and luxury. There is a large island with a waterfall marble countertop and on top of the island is a spread of munchies; fruits, cheeses, nuts, olives, salami, and crackers. I pick up a few olives and pop them in my mouth as Chandler starts walking down the hallway.

I quickly follow behind him and pass a dining room and glass doors leading to an office with floor-to-ceiling bookshelves and a view of the front yard through a big bay window.

I follow Chandler down the hall behind the family room and he opens the door to a guest room. Two twin over full bunk beds fill the space. He shrugs and says that this is where Nora and I will sleep and that the bunk beds are really only used when the whole family comes out.

He leaves and I unpack a bit and change into a swimsuit and coverup. Not sure if I'm getting in but I figured I'd try to look the part. I pick up my book but the effects of the coconut rum and no dinner linger so the words are still a little tricky to focus on. I toss it back on the bed and decide tonight is my fun night and that I'll lay low and read tomorrow.

I text a quick pic of our room to Nora and she tells me she's waiting for the bus and to have a drink ready for her when she arrives.

Is strip croquette a thing? Or is Adam just like fucking with me? It's hard to tell, also they're not identical but Adam is so obviously Chandler's twin that I feel kinda weird that he's flirting with me. Or messing with me. Because, no one has answered my inquiry about strip coquette.

It'd be weird if this was a game this family plays together. Like his cousins are here. I know Fiona is here with her girlfriend but it's still weird.

Right?

Yes.

Definitely.

"Whaddup bitches!!" Nora yells from the gate. And I am so glad for the excuse to leave Adam for a minute. I mean maybe when it rains it pours but first Jeff, now Adam and I've never had so much male attention in my life. All my 22 and a half years.

"Hey girl!" Oh that's the voice of Fun Liz. I guess those canned cocktails are adding up. "C'mon I'll show you to our room. Also, asking for a friend, is strip croquette a real game?"

"If not, it freaking is now! Sounds fun!"

Play Hard Nora, meet Fun Liz.

Fun Liz, meet Play Hard Nora.

It's about to go down.

CHAPTER 12

KYLE

Tiffany has her first work event tonight. It's a New York 30 Under 30 thing at Gracie Mansion. She said she was done around 10 and it's 10:30 now. The baseball game is over and I'm honestly feeling kind of tired but I don't want to go to bed if she's almost home.

My phone buzzes and I look down expecting it to be Tiffany and am surprised to see that it's Liz.

LIZ COLLINS: I feel like Chandler and Nora are going to have dirt on me after this weekend and I'm just glad you're not here so I might still be able to remain respectable in your eyes.

LIZ COLLINS: But now that I've actually sent that text I'm realizing you might figure out that I'm not cool at all and in fact lost so hard at strip croquette

LIZ COLLINS: Shit.

LIZ COLLINS: Now you know the dirt too.

I'm laughing to myself. I was ready with a response to her first text and then the other three came in short succession.

KYLE: Having a fun Friday night are we?

LIZ: Yes. Fun Liz came out to play tonight.

KYLE: Yeah? Is texting part of Fun Liz's agenda.

LIZ: Totes. She loves wearing a towel as a toga and texting while her adversaries set up another course.

The smile I'm sporting is stretching my cheeks out. I can feel the strain. I feel like teasing her but I don't want to do it over text, I want to be there in person. She's so fucking clever that conversation with her is easy and enjoyable. She gives as good as she gets.

KYLE: Sounds like a blast. Although, I'm more of a Bocce man myself.

LIZ: OMG same. Same my friend.

LIZ: Sorry to interrupt your night. I just wanted to make sure you wouldn't make fun of me for my terrible hitting a ball with a stick skills because I need at least one friend at Fosters.

KYLE: I won't make fun of you for that.

KYLE: And you're not interrupting my night at all.

LIZ: No? I thought you had a party tonight.

KYLE: Tiff does, I'm waiting for her to come home.

LIZ: Got it.

LIZ: Side note, there are a buttload of stars in the sky.

I can clearly picture her tipsy and lying on a lounge chair in a towel looking up at the sky.

And I feel a powerful urge to be with her.

Tiffany got home around 2:30. I had fallen asleep on the sofa after texting with Liz for another hour. First, about the stars then astrology and how much she believes in horoscopes and zodiac predictions. She skipped out on the next croquette match, challenged me to a bocce game, and then she heard a song she loved and we texted about music. I woke up when I heard the key in the lock and then Tiffany came in, said hi, and fell into bed where she passed out.

Already this morning I got up and went for a run while Tiffany slept. When I got back she was sitting up in bed on her phone. She smiled and then lazily made her way over to help me put my headphones away.

I didn't need the help but I welcomed it.

"Ewww, you're sweating" she says with a smile.

"Yes I am. I think I need a shower. What do you think?"

"I think you do. And you could probably use some help."

"Definitely."

"Okay, just a quick shower and then I've got to get to brunch. Oh a girl from work, Maddie, is having a birthday party tonight. I told her we'd be there."

I'm halfway through taking my shirt off when I pause. I hate clubs. There is absolutely no way I want to go to this party. I pull my shirt off the rest of the way to see Tiffany's naked backside slide through the bathroom door. As the shower turns on I remind myself that I decided to give this situation with Tiffany a shot. A relationship. And part of that is doing what she wants to do.

I hate this.
I tried to keep an open mind.
I tried to psych myself up for it.
C'mon Kyle, it'll be fun.
Be a young person and enjoy a night out at the club.
Enjoy being with your probably-should-put-a-label-on-it lady friend.
But, ugh.
We've only been here, checks watch, twenty minutes.
I fucking hate it.
Tiffany made me buy a new shirt for the party today and it's too tight.
I don't know anyone besides Tiffany.
The drinks are watered down.

From where I'm sitting at the table, alone, it seems like Tiffany is having a lot of fun dancing with her girlfriends from work. At least she's enjoying herself.

When she notices me sitting alone, she heads over and drags me out onto the dance floor.

"JUST ONE DANCE AND THEN YOU CAN GO!" she yells into my ear.

"ARE YOU GONNA STAY?" I yell back as she plugs her ear with a drink in her hand to block out the background noise.

"YEAH I THINK SO. THEN WE ARE GONNA GO TO THE NEXT CLUB." As she yells this, she starts to bounce to the beat.

"YEAH, I CAN'T DO ANOTHER CLUB." I try to stay close to her ear and end up bouncing myself.

"I KNOW BABE. THANKS FOR COMING. I'LL COME TO YOUR PLACE LATER!" and with that final yell she jumps back and starts bopping her head from side to side getting lost in the music.

I stay out on the dance floor for a few more renditions of the same song or maybe it's a new one. It is hard to tell when one song ends and the next begins. After that I give Tiffany a quick kiss on the cheek and head for the exit.

The club isn't that far from my apartment so I take advantage of the beautiful summer night and I walk home. I grew up in Connecticut, went to school in Connecticut too, so I've been to the city all my life but living here is different. I never knew what it was to walk for groceries or hear traffic and sirens all night long. It is equal parts exhilarating and exhausting.

I look up and can only see a few stars. I'm flooded with a feeling of nostalgia for the camping trip I took with my dad my senior year of high school. For the summers as a camp counselor. I miss being in the woods where you can see so many stars the sky looks like it's made of glitter.

My mind moves from remembering those nights to remembering Liz's comment from last night. My next thought is wondering how her day went. I want to call and find out. I want to talk to her.

For the next block I debate with myself.

One part of me is saying that I need to be loyal to Tiffany and not spend the night talking to another girl. Tiffany is, for all intents and purposes, my girlfriend even though I don't see it lasting much longer. Not when her idea of a fun time is one like tonight.

The other voice in my head is saying it can't hurt anyone to call Liz and see how her day was. To just talk. There's a good chance she doesn't even answer.

But wait, if she doesn't answer, do I leave a voicemail?

No one listens to their voicemails.

But a missed call with no message seems like a butt dial. When I am very much intending to talk to her.

It's another half block before I decide to text her.

CHAPTER 13

LIZ

Okay. I get it. I understand why everyone comes to the Hamptons. My skin is tight with salt and sun and wind and untangling my hair is going to take me a solid thirty minutes. But at the moment I don't care; I'm laying in the backyard on a towel staring up at the sky. There are so many freaking stars out again tonight that it reminds me of home.

At home we could see stars every night. I hadn't realized until tonight how little I look up at the sky anymore. I used to lay on a blanket in the backyard, just like this, reading by flashlight, and when my arms got tired from holding myself up I'd flip over on my back and just look up.

I'd get lost in daydreams. Visions of my big girl life in the city as a bad ass business woman. Of being married and kissing my husband and kids goodbye before hopping in the elevator which opens directly into our penthouse and then taking a town car to my office.

So far big city living hasn't been so glamorous but hopefully with a paycheck I can start building that vision. As a career woman I'll start by finding a better apartment. A studio of my own. Then I'll slowly build the wardrobe that every young professional woman should have. Quiet luxury styles of earth tones and clean lines. And once I have my housing under control and wake up every morning to a tidy and sophisticated wardrobe, I'm confident a boyfriend will come to me next.

Envisioning my life plans brings me back to those nights lying in the backyard looking up at the stars as a kid. I look up at the stars above me tonight. While I might feel like my life is chaotic and a hot mess, that little girl would probably be impressed with what I've got going for me.

I remind myself that each star is as big as our sun. Some are bigger. How many planets like ours are floating around their own suns? Is there a girl looking up at the stars on another planet? Is her hair as frizzy as mine? Has she figured out how to always dress appropriately for special functions?

Speaking of, I overpacked for this trip. I was channeling The Great Gatsby and brought fancy sundresses when everyone else was in their swimsuit and cover ups all day. I had those too but I'm a little sad about the dresses that are sitting rolled up in my bag.

I enjoyed the party last night but passed out on the sofa while texting Kyle. Don't worry, the white slipcovered overstuffed sofa is immensely more comfortable than the bed in my apartment. It felt like sleeping on a cloud. Nora hooked up with one of the guys last night which I discovered after I woke up early and went to get into my bed and was greeted with said guy's naked ass up in the air and Nora curled up next to him using her dress as a blanket. I snuck in to grab my toothbrush, book, and phone charger and snuck back out to the patio.

Within an hour there was a chef, Carolina, in the kitchen making omelets and pancakes and everyone slowly started to gather. By 10am the music was back on and morning drinks were passed around.

We migrated to the beach where I was able to take some photos but mostly I enjoyed having nowhere to go and nothing to do.

Tonight the party continues. Adam and Chandler actually hired a DJ and everyone is around the pool, still in their swimsuits, dancing, drinking, and squealing when someone gets pushed in.

I got my party fill last night and since no one seems to see me laying on the grass towards the back, I sneak inside and take a shower. Three rounds of conditioner was what it took for the the comb to slide through easily and my hair no longer resembles a rat's nest. Feeling fresh, I toss on one of my sundresses and grab my book.

Towards the front of the house there is an office that is lined with book filled shelves. There is a large writing desk up along one side of the room and on the other is another slipcovered, overstuffed sofa. I curl myself into the corner and excitedly open my book to start reading.

Vacation to me is a comfy chair and a romance novel.

The one I have with me this weekend promises a reunion between high school rivals. She left and went off to the big city. He came back after Med School and took over his dad's small medical practice in town. It's the high school reunion or something and they have to raise money for a new gym floor. The cover promises a baking scene.

I can't wait.

I was right. The rivals are in her family's kitchen baking for the cake walk fundraiser at the festival tomorrow and because of some merry mishap where the cakes she ordered got dropped during delivery. They're stealing glances and getting flour in each other's hair.

I'm smiling like a goon and giggling out loud to myself when my phone pings. I get the sense their first almost-kiss is coming and I want to savor that moment. That anticipation is building and you can feel the nerves the characters are experiencing. I hold my place with my finger and check my phone. It's a text from Kyle.

KYLE: Hey. Hope ur having fun in the Hamptons.

I slide my bookmark into place because I don't want my character's almost kiss to play second fiddle to Kyle. I could contribute my quickening heart rate to the story I'm reading but really it's every time I get to talk to him. I know he has a girlfriend and I never want to be the other woman but we're coworkers right? We can exchange friendly texts. No big deal.

LIZ: Hey! I am, although it's not the conventional definition of fun.

KYLE: Ha, what does that mean? I'm intrigued.

LIZ: It means I'm reading a romance novel in Chandler's dad's office slash library.

KYLE: No naked can jam tonight?

LIZ: That was this afternoon. My bits are sunburned.

Then the three dots appear. And disappear. And appear again. Shit. I've scared him off. I'm totally kidding, I didn't play naked anything today. We did play can jam at the beach today, with our swimsuits on, but I was terrible and decided to walk into town for iced coffee instead. I took my camera with me and got some really good stock photo images to sell. I'm excited to get home and edit them tomorrow night.

LIZ: Kidding.

LIZ: I had enough partying last night. But the embarrassment playing field was leveled when I walked in on Nora in bed with Chandler's brother and with Chandler getting hit in the face with a frisbee today.

KYLE: Well thank goodness for that.

LIZ: What are you up to?

KYLE: Walking home.

LIZ: From…

KYLE: A club. Tiffany's work friend was having a party so we went. It's not my scene so I left early.

I'm typing back "got it" when my phone rings. Kyle is calling me. I think it's a mistake so I decline it. Seriously, who talks on the phone? Then my hand starts ringing again.

"Are you seriously calling?" I say by way of answering the phone.

"I'm seriously calling. It's difficult to walk and text."

"Truth. I can't do two things at once."

"I heard a podcast that said 'single tasking' is better for your brain anyways." Of course he listens to life advice podcasts.

"That makes sense. So the club was a bust?"

"Yeah, I dunno. It isn't the crowd, I like being in a big crowd when it's a concert. It's the bad drinks and the bad music. I can't tell when the songs start and end."

I laugh. He sounds so old but also I totally understand what he's saying.

"I get that."

"So, you're reading now, you didn't get an inappropriate-to-talk about sunburn, what else did you do today?"

"I took my camera with me into town and got some good shots that I can sell to a stock photo site."

"I didn't know you did that. What were the pictures of?"

"Iced coffee."

He laughs and I smile feeling proud of myself for making him laugh.

"Seriously, your pictures were of coffee?"

"Yeah man. That shit sells! There are so many influencers that want pretty iced coffee shots that these sell like hotcakes. I add flowers in some, baked goods in others. But yeah one $6 iced coffee can get me like $60 in photo commissions."

"I had no idea."

"It's how I afford this affluent lifestyle."

He chuckles. "How long have you been doing it?"

"For a few years. I took a class called "graphic communication" and we learned about using stock photos in marketing materials. And then there was an assignment for taking stock style photos of our own. The ones I took were really good and the professor said I should upload them. I thought he was nuts, like who seriously pays for pictures of coffee when everyone has an iPhone in their pocket and can take one themselves. But I uploaded them and boom, my PayPal account overfloweth."

"Why aren't you taking photos full time?"

"Because that's not a job."

"What do you mean?"

"I mean, being a photographer isn't a good job. And I'm not good enough to be hired by a newspaper or magazine."

"Says who?"

"Says me."

"Well I don't know the first thing about art or photography but I gotta think that if your stuff is good enough to upload and sell then you're good enough to be a photographer. Or at least call yourself one."

"Yeah, I dunno, it's helping to pay the bills while I make copies for free this summer."

He laughs and the tension breaks. I was starting to squirm under his scrutiny of my photography. Or the idea of being a photographer.

"That does feel like all we're doing. Aunt Mary wanted me to get all this experience but I think the only thing I've learned so far is how to bind and ship paper."

"You've learned that everything should be freaking digital. Fosters might be the number one cause of deforestation."

He laughs. I smile.

"And going digital makes fixing mistakes easier."

"Hey now, we had a super fun bonding experience because of 'Danold Toff'! I learned all about the art of *Snackooterie* that night."

"That you did."

"Actually I bet the fridge here would be a *Snackooterie* chef's dream come true."

I'm rewarded again with his gentle laugh and I can picture that one dimple. I like talking to Kyle. He's genuinely interested in what I'm saying. He's kind. Thoughtful. If I didn't know he was dating someone I might think he was into me. But like, is that just because he's a guy showing interest? Like would I think anyone talking to me was into me?

This makes me think of when Nora said Marcus was flirting with me at the event last week. And then Jeff chatted me up at the bar and I freaking went home with him. And spent the weekend with him. And then had a first date, granted it was a double date, but we ate real date food.

Which, by the way, is Italian or French. Nothing hand held. Forks and knives means it's a date.

I haven't thought of texting Jeff once this weekend. He hasn't texted either. But I texted and talked on the phone with his unavailable best friend.

If I could afford it I'd sign up for therapy right now.

Obviously I've got some issues to work out.

CHAPTER 14

LIZ

The only new skill I learned this week was how to sweet talk a bike messenger into making my delivery first. Other than that it's been the same proofreading, copying, binding, and faxing of the last two weeks. The best part is hanging out in our Intern Cave. Think Man Cave but for people in uninspiring work conditions.

After Kyle and I talked for an hour on Saturday night we texted throughout the day Sunday. I showed him a few of my stock photos and he said his cousin Bryan totally uses one on his performance coaching website. He looked it up, sent me a screenshot, and sure as shit, there was a pic I took of a white oak desktop with a space gray keyboard, black coffee in a white mug, and black pen on a white lined notepad.

It was the first time I'd seen my work out in the real world. I do get the email addresses of people who buy my photos but I haven't tried to follow up with any of them. Seeing my picture on someone else's website made me proud and I think I stood a little straighter the rest of the day.

Now, it's Friday at 4pm and most of the consultants and partners have left for the day. Micro B is still here which is why the four of us are still here chatting quietly about what our plans are for the weekend. Chandler is going sailing with a buddy. Nora is, and I quote, going to "troll for some Financial District dick". I wish I had her balls.

Kyle said Tiffany had a party tonight so he's going to do laundry and chill to which both Nora and Chandler looked at him with pity. It sounded good to me because I needed to do laundry too. But since Kyle got such a bummer response from them I said "I don't really know yet, I'll see where the night takes me."

Nora and Chandler nodded their approval.

No response from Kyle.

Fine, whatever.

Turns out the night took me to the laundry room, then the corner liquor store for a bottle of rosé, then home to my room where I ate microwave popcorn for dinner, and watched rom coms on my computer.

The scene in Leap Year where she figures out he tricked her with the coin flip will forever be one of my favorites.

This morning hurts a little bit because of the almost full bottle of rosé I had with my popcorn but I'm still up and outside in clean clothes and waiting for Nora to show up. She texted last night that she didn't close her top prospect and so she was headed home to jill off. Forty-five minutes later she texted "we should hang out tomorrow, coffee at 10" and I replied "okie dokie" and she didn't respond until this morning suggesting a place.

"So, tell me about this boy last night." I ask because honestly I'm in awe of the fact that she'd approach a guy to try and pick him up. The only guys I've dated have approached me and even still I'm surprised I was able to seal the deal.

"Well first of all, he was a man. Thirty or thirty-one. I first noticed his watch when he handed his card to the bartender. I kept my eye on him for a bit and then walked over and started asking about his job."

I'm completely enraptured by this story already. "Then what?"

"He started talking about this big deal he closed and how he went out and celebrated it at this club in the meatpacking district."

"I will always laugh like a twelve year old boy hearing the word 'meatpacking'."

"Hard not to. I wanted to show him I was interested so I started to do stuff like touch his arm or brush up against him when someone walked behind me. But he didn't respond at all. No smiles, no eye contact. Nothing. So I thought he was maybe shy. I started to drop not-subtle hints like that I was getting tired and might head home to bed soon. And then he said 'Nice to meet you Nola.' and walked away."

"Ouch! Brutal."

"I know. Douche. He was so hot though. I had a nice night with my vibrator but I need a rebound tonight."

"Well I am not good at picking guys up but I would be willing to tag along." Then an idea struck me. "You remember that bar we went to a few weeks ago with Kyle. They have live music on Saturday nights. That could be fun!"

"Yeah, and totally different vibe than last night so let's see how I do there. And why do you say you're not good at picking up guys?"

"Because I'm not. I get all awkward and nervous."

"Jeff took you home right? And Marcus was totally hitting on you at work."

"Agree to disagree about Marcus but Jeff pursued me. I do ok if they're the ones leading the evening."

"Into the alphas then? BDE all day. Stick with me girl, I'll show you how it's done. Okay, what are you going to wear?"

"Probably what I always wear. Jean shorts, t-shirt and sneakers. Maybe a band shirt since it's a live music night. I haven't put much thought into it."

The look Nora gives me down her nose and over the tops of her sunglasses is startling. Her eyes are absolutely piercing me with disdain. I'm immediately wondering what I've done wrong.

"No." She says as she pushes her sunglasses back up her nose. "I will not let you wear jean shorts and a t-shirt to a bar on a Saturday night. Throw the men a bone and wear a bodysuit or a dress." Nora stops walking suddenly and pivots towards me. "Follow me." And she starts walking in the direction we came from.

"Hold up, where are you going?"

"Shopping."

"Nora, no. This is outrageous." It's only half an hour later and I'm holding up a sundress on a hanger outside a dressing room.

Actually, "dress" is an exaggeration, this is a flowy scrap of fabric. It's a sunny yellow color which I love but also low cut with a shirred top which I don't.

It is a departure from my usual t-shirt and jeans.

Like total detour.

"Just try it on. If you do and hate it you can wear your grimiest t-shirt out tonight and I won't say a word."

"Promise?"

"Promise."

"You're on."

CHAPTER 15

KYLE

When Jeff and I were undergrads we figured out pretty quickly that we both loved music. We were constantly discovering new bands and learning new songs to play ourselves. Jeff plays guitar and can sing decently. I've been playing bass since middle school. We met Chris, our drummer, when he heard us playing through my dorm window and he came inside and found us. We learned a bunch of cover songs together, wrote a few originals of our own, and have been playing here and there for a few years. It wasn't until a month ago that Jeff put us on the list to play at Cooper's live music nights.

This is our second time playing here. The first time was nerve wracking but really fun. It's a good crowd tonight and I'm excited. Still a bit nervous but excited.

We named our band "Free Beer" in the hope that the MC would announce us to the crowd like "Okay everyone, put your hands together, it's time for FREE BEER!"

I place an order for a soda water with lime and turn around and lean back on the bar to scan the room. I don't see anyone I recognize. That's good. It's more awkward to play songs in front of people you know. It's more intimate.

I'm turning back towards the bar when two girls walk in and I do a double take. They're stopped by Gus at the door to show ID so they turn around and I don't get to see their faces. One of them is in a yellow dress and from behind I can only describe her as hot.

Hotter when she bends down because she dropped her ID and her skirt lifts up to where her ass meets her thighs. I follow the line of her legs down, they're lean but strong and I stop when I catch the ribbon tied around her ankle holding her wedge sandals in place.

I can appreciate the finer details of summer footwear because of the hours I put in as Tiffany's outfit sounding board this week. I don't understand why girls toddle around in those things but they're helping her legs look so irresistible that I'll never question it again.

Her hair is down in loose brown curls and they bounce as she throws her head back to laugh at something Gus said after checking her ID.

"Here's your club soda kid. Break a leg."

I grab my drink and by the time I turn back around to the girls they've made their way to the other end of the bar and are out of sight. It's for the best. Show starts in 5 minutes.

We killed it. The energy was electric and people were digging the originals. We mixed them in with covers. Jeff even had the highlight of his career when he announced "one last original" before we launched into Mr. Brightside by The Killers. I could see the doubt in the crowd's faces turn to joy when they realized they'd been duped.

Yellow Dress Girl was in the back. With the lights on the stage I couldn't really see her face but I kept an eye on her best I could. She and her friend were bouncing along and ordering drinks. I assume they enjoyed the show.

"Hey losers! Nice job!" a familiar voice calls from behind me. I turn and see Nora approaching. Then from behind her comes Liz, in a yellow dress.

Jeff responds first because my mouth has gone dry.

"Hey! Thanks for coming!"

"Yeah, it took this one," Nora throws a thumb over her shoulder at Liz, "a little longer than usual to get out of the house. And imagine our surprise when you guys ended up on stage!"

"Yeah total shocker!" Liz says. "I thought we'd be meeting you here to watch the band. Not watching you be the band. It was such a great set!"

And she reaches forward to hug Jeff, then Chris, who is still holding his drum sticks, and then she turns to me. Her smile is huge as she leans towards me for a hug.

Her arms wrap around my neck and mine find their way around her body. She is warm and my hand splays out a little more to capture as much of her feel as I can. Her chest is pressed up against mine and the pressure is electric, buzzing with energy. She had to go up on her tiptoes so as we release the hug she bounces back to the ground.

My hand is still on the small of her back after the hug and I have to tell myself to let go.

"So glad you came. What a surprise." I manage to say as we step back from each other.

Liz seems to be a little dazed. Her eyes are big and round and full of questions when she turns up to look at my face. She blinks, twice, and then seems to come out of her trance. "Where's Tiffany?" she asks with a cough like she got the words stuck in her mouth.

"She's working. Might come by later."

"Cool. Well, let's get a drink." And she gives Nora a look of some sort and then Nora flashes her gaze to me for a split second.

"Shut up, you did not."

"Ha, I totally did." I'm telling Liz about the time that Jeff and I had planned to drive to Florida for spring break in a camper van that we rented with some other friends. Well, long story short I was driving overnight and everyone else was sleeping. Even Jeff who had promised that he'd stay up and keep me company. I stopped for gas, no one stirred, and then I got back on the freeway but I was going the wrong direction. After four hours I realized that we were halfway back to Connecticut so I got off the freeway, turned around and drove south again. When people woke up they wondered why we hadn't made better time and I made up some excuse about crazy weird traffic instead of admitting that I had gone four hours out of the way.

"So did they believe you?"

"Probably not, but again, I was the one who volunteered for the night shift so they let it slide."

"That's so great. What an adventure! I don't have any adventure stories.

My life has been so boring."

"I doubt that. You left your hometown and went to Brown, that's an adventure."

"True, but Brown seems like small potatoes when your siblings went to Harvard and Dartmouth. And especially when I floated the idea of an art degree! That did not go over well." She says with a shake of her head.

"Do your parents expect you to follow a certain career path? Or do what your siblings are doing?"

"Not exactly. But it's implied. There's a lot of 'Well Charlie Jr is making the family proud over at Amherst Regional' or 'Maggie is doing blah blah blah now and plans to be a prosecutor before too long'." She says in a fake bravado voice and ends with a shrug.

I can understand how her wanting to be in the arts after her older brother and sister went the power-suit route would seem like a subpar choice to some people. My parents put me in all sorts of activities but sports were prioritized over art classes when I was younger. It wasn't until I started playing guitar and bass in my middle school music class that they invested in lessons for me.

But it also was never discouraged. My mom took pottery classes with her girlfriends. My dad did handy stuff around the house. And we were outdoors a lot as a family. From what it sounds like Liz was kind of lonely as a child. With two siblings that are much older I can see how that happens.

I was an only child but I don't feel like I was ever lonely.

Especially with my cousins just down the road.

"I never had to compete for affection, being an only child, but I do have cousins that I got to mess around with and who helped pave the way for me."

"See, my brother and sister were probably more like cousins to me. Both my parents were only children so there weren't any cousins around."

"That's too bad. I remember once when Bryan and I stole his dad's car for a fishing trip. We had it packed up with all the gear and then when we went to park it by the pier–"

Liz's eyes flash to something behind me and go wide. I'm turning to look for myself when my head is smothered in a hug.

"Baby!"

Tiffany reaches her arms around me and kisses me and then slaps her bag down on the table and sets her phone on top of it. She stands back up and walks to the bar to order a drink. Liz and I just look at each other, unsure about what to do after that interruption, when Tiffany's phone pings. It's instinct to look at a phone when it sounds the alert. I can see the screen because it's right under my nose.

BadBoy: You better not have washed me off yet.

I'm trying to figure out what that means when it pings again.

BadBoy: I haven't washed you off.

What the fuck?

I grab the phone and stand so quickly my chair topples backwards and crashes to the ground. I march up to the bar. I hear Liz say my name with concern in her voice but it sounds like it's miles away or coming from behind glass. Tiffany and I are not in a relationship but I've been not making a move on Liz for the last few weeks thinking that I owe Tiffany something. Loyalty maybe? But DTR conversation or not, she's clearly hooking up with someone else.

I'm seeing red.

"What the fuck is this?" I demand.

"Huh?" Tiffany turns with her vodka soda in hand "What are you talking about? Why do you have my phone?"

"Who is 'BadBoy'?"

"Oh, Kyle, that's umm, it's nothing"

"Doesn't look like *nothing*. Looks like you slept with him tonight."

"What are you talking about?!"

I hand her the phone and she sees the texts on the preview screen. She knows. I can see her wheels turning trying to spin this. Always the public relations professional.

"Ky, it's just some guy. We didn't sleep together, just mouth stuff."

"Why do you think that's better!?" I spin around with my hands clasped on the back of my head. I take a step away but stop and pivot back towards her. "We're done."

"Kyle. C'mon. We can figure this out."

"I don't want to figure this out. We're finished."

I think about waiting to watch her leave. To watch her sulk out like a wounded animal but I'm twitching with anger and I have to get out of there. I turn back to the table and Liz is standing there with a look of concern in her eyes. I can't think straight. The walls are closing in on me.

Liz smiles at me as she walks around the table and I can feel myself offer her a sad smile back. I was having such a good time until Tiffany showed up. I hear Tiffany say my name and I know I have to get out of here. I brush past Liz to head backstage for my stuff. She reaches out and touches my arm to try and stop me. But I can't have her pity. I desperately want her to be the one to comfort me in this moment but it can't be from a place of pity. I'll never be able to move past being the wounded animal in her eyes. We'll be stuck in that dynamic.

When Liz turns and takes a step to follow me she wobbles on her heels and slips, falling flat on that ass I was admiring earlier.

I rush back to her side and help her stand up. "You okay?"

"Yeah, I'm fine. Silly me. Okay. Thanks. I'm so sorry Kyle. Umm, I gotta go." It looks like she could start crying.

We stand there frozen for a minute holding a conversation with our eyes. I open my mouth to tell her that I had fun tonight even though it ended badly but before I can say anything she turns towards the door and walks away. I watch her leave and then head backstage. Ignoring Tiffany completely.

CHAPTER 16

LIZ

I have a giant bruise on my ass and that dress I ended up liking has a giant gray bar sludge spot from where I fell. What had been a surprisingly fun night turned terrible in the blink of an eye.

Kyle and I were having a great conversation. We enjoy the same movies and TV shows and music although he knows way more music than I do. He was interested in learning more about my family. He was flirty and listened when I spoke and I completely forgot he was dating Tiffany until I saw her walk up behind him.

Then I guess they broke up.

Shrug Emoji?

I'm not totally sure what happened but Kyle was clearly angry and hurt. I wanted to comfort him, be there for him, talk with him, be a friend. But he pushed me away. I could see him shutting down. Then when I tried to reach out to him I lost my balance and fell.

Instantly he turned protective and reached out to help me when all I wanted was to be able to help him. I was mortified. Not only did I fall in front of him, a guy I've started to like, but I also fell in front of his beautiful girlfriend, or ex-girlfriend. And I'll have to see him back at the office tomorrow.

I can feel myself starting to spiral in shame when my phone pings.

NORA: Ummm, yeah, hi. I know you hooked up with Jeff like two weeks ago and I asked you if it was OK last night. Hoes before Bros for life. But, seriously, is this gonna be a problem?

LIZ: Nope! He's all yours. Although I thought I was the one who needed a hook up.

NORA: I stand by that. You do.

NORA: Wait, you didn't go home with Kyle last night?

LIZ: Nope. Just fell on my ass walking out of the bar after witnessing him break up with Tiffany.

NORA: OMG no way. I can't believe I missed that. I'll be over in an hour. We'll discuss over bagels.

LIZ: Hurry.

Nora and I ventured to midtown to get bagels and iced coffee. She dished about Jeff and I kept asking her questions until she figured out I was deflecting.

"I cannot believe I wiped out. Ugh. Brutal." I'm hiding my face in my hands. "Did I tell you about wiping out before my Fosters interview?"

"What? No! How did I not know about this."

"Ohmigod. It was bad. I was feeling so confident. I marched into the lobby in my cutest kitten heels. I had my bag slung over my shoulder and I had just gotten my pass from security. I walked through the gate thing and I turned to say thank you to the security guard and I skidded out on my heel. Kersplat. Somehow I landed on my knee and went down on my side. My bag slid to the other side of the elevator lobby. Two guys were getting out of an elevator. One helped me stand up and the other grabbed my bag. I think I heard one of them say 'ouch, that's gotta hurt.' I quipped 'Well they better give me the job now' and ran into an open elevator before I could start crying. It's a miracle I kept my composure in that interview."

"Liz, that's so crazy." She pauses and turns towards me. "Wait, is this why you never wear heels at work?"

I bite off a chunk of bagel. "Bingo." I say with my mouth full.

Nora takes this all in over sips of iced coffee and we stride further into the park.

"So what exactly happened with Kyle?"

"We were having so much fun. I seriously forgot he had a girlfriend until I saw her walking in. Is that bad? Does that make me a bad woman? Like I don't respect girl code or something?" Nora just shrugs. Not helpful. "Well anyway, she tossed her bag on the table and walked to get a drink. Her phone buzzed and he saw something on her phone and stormed up to her at the bar. All I heard him say was "we're done" and then he walked back towards the table. He didn't say anything else to me so I really have no idea what's going on. Then I fell, he helped me up, and I ran out of there as fast as I could."

I gotta stop talking because as I do I relive it and it is making me cringe and almost cry. I blink hard a few times, suck in a breath and go back into deflection mode. "So when are you gonna see Je-ehhhhhh-ff again?" I string his name out like I'm about to start a lively rendition of Jeff and Nora sitting in a tree, K-I-S-S-I-N-G.

Nora takes a giant bit of bagel, rolls her eyes but can't hide her smile.

"Ohmygosh you like him! Maybe you *like* him like him!"

"Ha, nah, liking guys isn't my thing. It was fun."

We finish our bagels and cold brews and decide to continue our walk through the park.

CHAPTER 17

KYLE

A run was a good idea. Feels good. It is a perfect day and the park is busy. Sometimes the crowds bother me but today it was comforting to know there is a world of people out there who don't care about me breaking up with my maybe girlfriend Tiffany and instantly crushing hard on Liz.

I can now say that yes, I've been crushing on Liz, for longer than I care to admit.

After the initial anger passed of catching Tiffany getting dirty texts from another guy, I decided I was glad this happened. I probably wouldn't have broken up with Tiffany otherwise. The other thought I had was how badly I wish I had walked Liz home.

Now it feels weird. Like Liz will probably expect me to be upset and not interested in anyone else so soon. Is there a way for me to tell her that I've been interested since I saw her in April? That I hadn't cheated on Tiffany. I just kind of forgot that I was dating someone? But I'd never do that to her because she's something else entirely. And, no I don't know what exactly that something else is but I've never felt it before.

I'm talking in circles. And running in circles. I think I've gone down the same path twice now. I must be doing a loop through the park because usually I cut straight through and continue to the riverwa—

"OOH ACK!"

"Oh shit! I'm sorry!" I manage to sputter as I stumble over the person I just collided with.

"What the hell?" I look up and it's Nora. I glance down as the brunette on the ground starts to stand up.

Liz.

LIZ

"OOH ACK!"

"OH shit! I'm sorry!"

I recognize that voice.

"What the hell?" Nora belts out.

I look up and meet Kyle's surprised gaze.

"Liz! I'm so sorry! I was lost in thought and didn't see you."

"Obviously. No, it's fine. No big deal. My fault." I manage to get out before the embarrassment blooms up my cheeks.

"No. Totally my fault." He is bending down to meet my gaze so show me how sincere he's being. Damn it. That's a romance hero move. And who knew he was so tall? It's not noticeable in the way some freakishly tall guys are but he's the right kind of tall.

The have-to-get-on-my-tiptoes-to-hug-around-the-neck kind.

Like I did last night when we first saw them after the show. I felt so proud of him for going up there and playing and showing off his talents. And, holy mother of macaroni that hug was incredible. His arms felt so sturdy around me, his hands held me with this sensational combination of strength and tenderness. I was pressed up against his chest, feeling my heart race, and telling myself under no circumstances could I kiss him.

But, let me tell you, I wanted to kiss him.

And now he's just a few inches from my face and I am thinking about kissing him.

Cue red cheeks.

"Are you okay?" He takes a half a step back and scans my body holding my biceps at arm's length. His fingers radiating heat. "Is your knee bleeding?"

"Oh shit, yeah, your knee is bleeding." Nora chimes in.

I give her a look that says 'not helpful'.

And, speaking of not helpful. Universe, seriously?

Why can't I be graceful around this guy? I'd settle for steady on my feet if graceful isn't on the menu. Anything to not be the one constantly falling down and needing first aid.

"C'mon, my place is just two blocks that way." He says while pointing west. "Let's go and get it cleaned up."

Kyle looks genuinely concerned and, okay fine, I like having his attention focused on me a little bit, and I like feeling his hands on me a lotta bit.

KYLE

Luckily I'm a pretty tidy guy so the girls can come into my place and not be disgusted. And, actually it'll just be a quick clean up of Liz's knee and then they'll leave.

Because simply having Liz in the lobby of my apartment building set my pulse to racing.

Now that we're walking down the hall to my door I can feel sweat gathering at my brow. It's definitely from the run I was on right before this. Not nerves.

"Right through here," I say as I hold open the door for them.

"So this is where you live huh?" Nora says, taking a noisy slurp of coffee while surveying the place and plopping her purse on the counter like she's been here a million times before. Liz hobbles to the stool at the kitchen counter and perches on the edge.

"This is it. In all its glory. I'll grab my first aid kit. Be right back."

LIZ

He's touching my knee.

No, more accurately he's touching the back of my knee while he uses a damp paper towel to clean out my scrape.

And now he's blowing on my knee to dry it.

My head feels light.

I can now completely understand the moments in period piece movies where a man touches a woman's ankle and she basically loses her virginity on the spot. I get it.

"What are you up to tonight?" Nora, thankfully, is blissfully unaware of my nerves being on high alert and Kyle's touch doing things to my head. And body.

"I don't have any plans." Did he just glance up at me?

I've gotta stop with the romance novels.

"Jeff just texted and I think I'm going to head over to his place. Order in and watch a movie or something." She shrugs. "His dad gets him all the fancy subscriptions so we could pick almost anything."

"Did Jeff invite us or just you-uuu?" I make it sing-songy and I notice a huff of laughter from Kyle. I smile with pride because I made him laugh.

"I told him that Kyle ran into us, literally, and that we were back at his place and that we should all hang out tonight so yeah, ya nerd, he invited all of us."

"Sounds like fun. What time?" Kyle says as he applies the bandaid and follows it with a touch to the inside of my knee that was so soft that I might have imagined it.

Except I have to grab onto the stool with both hands so I don't tip over.

CHAPTER 18

KYLE

Pizza and a movie with Liz, Nora, and Jeff was a lot of fun. We picked a movie we'd all seen before so we joked around and talked the whole time. I learned that Liz can't wink with both eyes; only her right. She learned that I once lost a bet and had to streak through freshman orientation. We learned that Nora once drove a riding lawn mower to school when her parents hid her keys because she missed curfew.

When the movie was over Liz and I walked out together because Nora was giving Liz wiggly eyebrows. I pretended not to notice. I don't know if the eyebrows were for Liz and me or Nora and Jeff.

As we took the elevator down to the lobby I had to fight every cell in my body not to ask Liz to come home with me. Or invite myself to go home with her. Since literally running into her earlier in the day all I could think about was having the chance to call myself her boyfriend. I went to sleep last night picturing her face as she laughs. I woke up with the phantom feel of her body next to mine.

Nora got called into a meeting right when she got to the office today and we haven't seen her since. Chandler is in the corner with headphones on proofreading something. Liz and I are doing an online search for our clients to pull press about their programs. The idea being we can focus on the geographical areas these outlets distribute to and grow the donor base.

She keeps kind of looking across the table at me and I feel her head lift so I look up and then we both look away quickly. That's a sign she's into me right? Or is she still wondering how I'm doing after the break up?

"Okay, I can't sit here any longer and not ask," she says, looking up at me and folding her arms in front of her on the table.

Shit, here it comes. She's going to ask about the breakup and I don't want to be callous about it because I am a caring person, I just don't care so much about Tiffany.

"Do you want to go get a coffee?" Liz smiles at me and I laugh because I think she knew I was bracing to talk about my feelings.

"Yeah, from the breakroom or the deli?"

"Deli. I found three more articles than you did so you're buying." She says while pointing a finger gun in my direction. It's awkward and cute and totally her.

Liz and I are walking back into the lobby when she turns towards me and finally asks what I expected her to.

"How are you doing buddy?" She says as she throws a punch at my arm.

Worse now that she called me *buddy*.

"Honestly, fine. Tiffany and I had been kind of drifting apart anyways and so this just pushed us apart for good."

"Have you talked to her?"

"No. She texted a few times that night and then called yesterday but there's nothing to say."

"You don't need closure?" She asks as we step into the elevator and turn towards the doors.

"Nah, it's pretty clean cut."

Someone throws their arm into the closing doors to stop them. We both look and see Marcus proudly standing on the other side.

"Hello." He says while looking straight at Liz. "What a lovely surprise to find you in the elevator!"

"Hey Marcus. Kyle and I were just taking a quick break from finding articles but we're headed right back there now to keep searching."

"Oh, I don't care. That's a busy work task we give you when there's nothing else going on. We normally don't even do anything with the data you collect."

Well that sucks to know.

"That's too bad. There's a compelling story with some of these articles." Liz replies.

I sneak a glance at Liz behind Marcus's back. He's between us in the elevator but he's facing forward. I can tell she's trying to stifle a laugh.

"Is there now?" Marcus turns towards her. "Maybe you can come to my office and share these compelling stories."

I see her cheeks flush. "Of course, just tell me when."

"I'll double check my calendar but let's say 5 tonight."

"Oh, sure. Yes. Sounds good."

Five tonight? He's asking her to come to his office to work but it feels like he's asking her out on a date. It's in his tone. And I know she was bullshitting him with the compelling story stuff because the articles we've found have been dull and a few have been mostly copied from a press release our client sent out. The bylines change but the material doesn't.

As soon as we're down the hallway and back in the conference room Liz sits down and starts working again. She's avoiding eye contact with me. After a few minutes she hangs her head and lets out a huff of air.

"I'm so fucked."

"No you're not." I offer.

"What do you mean?" Chandler asks.

"Marcus basically told Kyle and I that we were doing pointless busywork and I wanted to prove that our time was worth something so I told him we had found some interesting information. When in reality this project is completely pointless and I'm going to have to walk in there at 5 and tell him so."

"Ha, yeah, you're fucked."

"Shut up Chandler." She crumples up a sheet of paper and tosses it at him. "Ugh, what am I going to do?"

"Do what I do." Chandler says confidently.

"And what's that exactly?"

"I use jargon phrases like 'based on my first pass' or 'this might need to go on the backburner for now' or 'we can circle back to this later once I've had a chance for a deep dive'. It's all the bullshit sayings that I hear my dad use. They feel like I know what I'm talking about without ever giving them any actual information."

"That's not a terrible idea." I shrug and look at Liz.

"All the synergy in this room is pumping me up for my meeting." She says with a smile.

Liz didn't ask me to wait for her after the meeting with Marcus but I wanted to. I could see her get more and more nervous as the afternoon went on. She masked it by making jokes and practicing her jargon talk. I also saw her making a few notes from the articles so maybe she did figure something out after all.

While I wait I have time to think. About Liz. How soft her leg was. The goosebumps that ran down her skin when I was patching her up. How I stole a few extra milliseconds of contact after I applied the bandaid.

I wanted to pull her legs to my waist and eliminate all the space between us.

Maybe I can walk her home tonight. We could stop for dinner. Or I could cook for her at my place. I know she's got that stoner roommate and she never talks about cooking herself dinner. She also swipes a lot of those fruit and nut bars from the breakroom.

I'm thinking through the ingredients I have in the fridge when I see her walk out the door. She spots me and smiles. I stand up from where I was leaning against a pillar in the lobby and walk towards her.

"Hey Ky. You didn't have to wait for me."

"I wanted to know how it went. So, tell me how it went." I nudge her with my elbow and she leans to the side and beams. I could stare at that smile for hours.

"I kind of hate to admit it but Chandler's Jargon Method worked. I couldn't believe it. After a few sentences I almost started laughing because Marcus was buying it so hard!"

"Maybe you should go into sales."

"Maybe." She says as she smiles to herself.

We walk a few more blocks together without saying anything. I go from thinking it is wonderfully comfortable to thinking it is painfully awkward. When I'm feeling the latter I clear my throat or say umm or cough and I see her smile out of the corner of my eye and I start sliding back towards the comfortable side of the scale.

We stop at a red light and she looks up at me. I can see her mind working and the conversations she's having in her head are displayed in the subtle changes in her eyes. She inhales and levels her chin.

"I'm gonna head home. Thanks again for staying, it was nice to have a walking home buddy for a few blocks. Have a good one!"

And she waves over her shoulder as she rushes across the street before the light changes.

I stand on the corner for a beat and watch her float down the sidewalk. I hate that she's walking away. That I didn't speak up to ask her over for dinner. That I don't know what she's going to do when she gets home. That I am drawn to her but have no idea if she's drawn to me.

CHAPTER 19

LIZ

"Everybody get this." Chandler is looking at his phone. I'm expecting that there's been some sort of national news event so I pick up my phone and open the news app.

"My parents have offered the house to Adam and I next weekend. Fourth of July at the Hamptons House Bay-BEE!" Chandler holds out knuckles to Kyle who obliges.

"Yes! I'm in," Nora confirms instantly.

I catch Kyle's eye. We haven't done anything to make us a couple but we've connected on a different level the past few days. Or maybe it was the same level it has always been just now he's technically available so my mind has opened up to the idea.

And now it's running away with the idea of being away in the Hamptons with him. Even on a group trip there could be plenty of one-on-one time. I haven't seen Kyle in resort wear yet but based on how he rocks a suit for the office and a black tee and jeans for a show it's easy enough for me to envision a linen button down shirt that's open at the top with trunks and aviators. I almost have to slurp to keep my drool in my mouth.

Something in his eyes change and I'm wondering what is going through his mind. I'm not going to pass up the opportunity to hang out with him so I've got to make a quick phone call and reschedule my parent's visit.

Once I'm down the hall I call my mom.

"Helloo Lizzard! What a surprise to hear from you!"

"Hi Mom."

"Why are you so quiet? Is everything okay? Do I need to call the police? Drop a pin and I'll run next door and have Jenny tell me what to do with that."

"No, Mom, I'm fine," I can hear the screen door slap closed in the background. She's already running next door. "I'm just at work and don't want to be too loud in the hallway."

"Oh, thank goodness." Then there is a muffled noise over the speaker and I hear her say "False alarm Jenny, everything's okay." Then she comes back. "So, what's going on darling?"

"I was wondering if you and Dad could come another time? I just got invited to a friend's house in the Hamptons for the weekend and I kinda want to go."

"What friend is this? That Charles person you work with?"

"Chandler. And yes. It's his parent's house again."

"Well your Father already bought tickets to a show for Friday afternoon. Can you go to your friend's house on Saturday and we'll just cut the visit short by a day?"

"I think that could work. Thank you."

"Of course sweetie. We want you to have as much fun this summer as you can. We're excited to see what you're up to in the city and to bring you some food from the garden."

"No, don't worry about the food. I honestly don't cook so it would go to waste."

"What! What do you mean you don't cook? What are you eating?"

"Mom, I can't have this conversation right now. We'll talk when you get here on Thursday night. I love you, bye!"

I rush off the phone as I hear her saying "bye" because if I didn't end the call I would have been there for another twenty minutes detailing my diet which is basically bagels, coffee, and protein bars. While my parents can be annoying, and set high expectations, they really are cool and the fact that she just offered to leave a day early is a testament to that. Also I'm sure she's less than thrilled about staying at my place. I've offered to take the sofa and I've bribed my roommate not to smoke at home this week with $50 cash from my stock photo sales.

Back in the conference room they're still talking about the Hamptons and Chandler is explaining to Kyle and Nora who all will be there.

"I'm in but only for Saturday. My parents are coming to town Thursday so they're going to stay until Saturday morning and then I'll head out."

"Awesome. This is going to be such an epic weekend."

I can't help but look at Kyle again, he smiles in a small but significant way and, yeah, this is going to be an epic weekend indeed.

Interns are generously allotted two vacation days all summer. I used one today and did all the touristy things with my parents. They got in last night and after bringing their bags upstairs I gave them a quick tour, there isn't much to see anyways, and then I took them to a South American restaurant down the street.

The show my dbought tickets for today was an artist immersive experience and it was only 45 minutes so we had time to walk the Brooklyn Bridge, hang out in Dumbo, visit the Fruit Streets, a farmers market, and walk along the water. We made our way over to Park Slope and my dad waited on the curb while my mom and I explored The Ripped Bodice bookstore. It's 4pm and I've officially run out of funtivities. We're sitting at our second coffee shop of the day sipping iced coffees. Well, technically my mom has iced tea and my dad has water but I'm drinking the sweet nectar that is cold brew. It's getting awkward though and I don't think I can fill the next 6 hours until bedtime.

I haven't brought up photography because it's a non-starter with my dad. It's just not a "real job" in his mind. However, my camera is in my bag today and I've been able to snap a few photos while my parents popped in and out of stores. I took a few of them when they weren't paying attention and even without pulling them up on my computer I can tell they're going to be full of affection.

My parents have a strong relationship. Something to strive towards. They supported one another as they both earned advanced degrees. My Mom is a surgical nurse who works at the hospital. My Dad is a retired research scientist and tenured professor. He worked in a lab at the university a few towns over and still teaches one class a semester. His name is on a few studies that were in the running for nobel prizes.

Both are from very scientific, standard process heavy, detail oriented jobs. My siblings followed suit.

It was tough when Margaret left for college and I was starting 7th grade. It felt good to get their full attention for a while. And things were pretty good between me and my parents all through high school and into college until I floated the idea of a photography and graphic design career when home for winter break my junior year. I had just added photography as an official minor and had made a few stock photo sales. My courses were selected for the second semester but I was thinking about what I would take my senior year and wanted to talk it through with my parents.

I remember starting the conversation, Dad immediately shutting the idea down, my Mom trying to keep me from storming off to my room right before I went storming off to my room. As I was doing it I felt full of high school angst again but I didn't even want to start down *The Path*.

You know the one, where my dad reminds me how much he's invested in my education. The same amount he invested in Charlies's pre-med degree, the same amount invested in Margaret's pre-law degree. When I suggested public policy I knew he'd see it as my pre-presidental degree or something.

I did well enough in high school and with my AP Classes I got an over 4.0 GPA. College was going fine too because I learned how to appease the instructors of the classes I struggled in. Like if I asked Mr. Lee for help with one part of a statistics problem he'd take the time to walk through the entire thing and inadvertently ended up giving me all the answers.

For my dad though, you get an education, the best one money can buy, and then you get a high paying job to pay him back for the education he bought you. I worked all through college and was able to keep my balance with him reasonable. Even though photography is something I love I can't rely on it for enough income to support myself.

So, that night, I sat in my room and scrolled through social media for hours and actually came up with more ideas for stock photos based on what bloggers were posting.

The next morning Mom was able to tell me the summarized version of what Dad had bellowed last night. That they just want what's best for me, they want me to have job security, that they want me to use the marketing and public policy degrees I was earning too. And if I wanted to do 'the photography as a little hobby' then I certainly could.

My photography instructor was disappointed that I wasn't taking the advanced portrait class he had talked to me about but he said he understood. He also told me not to let my parents decide these things for me but I know better than to bite the hand that feeds you.

So here I am a few years later, an intern at a development consulting firm trying to convince my parents that these eight weeks of unpaid labor will pay off in the long run. That I'll either land a job at Fosters or an even better one at a high profile organization. That this is the start of a life-long prestigious career.

My heart is just not in it though.

Sure we're doing grunt work at Fosters this summer and my dreams never included the amount of faxing I've done but even when I do deliver or contribute I don't feel validated. I don't get excited about it. Even in the last few weeks I've noticed my motivation sliding.

Honestly, I think I'm motivated to do well with Kyle more than anything. He's turned out to be a pretty good friend. I thought this internship would be competitive and that I'd be on my own to impress the Fosters team. But Kyle isn't competitive that way. Maybe it's because has a job with his Aunt but I also just don't see him being ruthless or selfish.

When I told Kyle about the photography I was surprised by his instant and unquestioning support. By his optimistic attitude. We'd known each other for like a week. For a moment I've forgotten where I am and I am back in that library on the phone with Kyle. My mouth turns into a smile while I replay our phone call from a few weeks ago. My cheeks flush as I think about his hands on my leg last weekend.

Mom totally catches it.

"What, or who, has you smiling like that Liz?"

"Huh? Oh, nothing."

"It's not nothing."

"No, it's not, but I don't know what it *is*," which is God's honest truth. I don't know what's going on. I think he's into me but he could also just be a really nice guy. I know I feel more confident when I'm around him. That I look forward to seeing him every morning and miss talking to him at night. That making him laugh sets off sparklers in my bloodstream.

"Well, if whoever it is can make you smile like that just thinking about them it's worth figuring out what it is."

Mom lays that sage wisdom out on the table and takes a sip of her iced tea. Dad is reading the newspaper. I feel myself stand up before I register the thought that I want to stand.

"Are we leaving?" Dad asks.

"Umm, I…" I need to get to the Hamptons and see Kyle. "Yeah, I think we are. Can you give me a ride to the Hamptons?"

CHAPTER 20

KYLE

"Boys trip!!" I hear as a pair of hands come clapping down on my shoulders. I don't have to turn around to know it's Chandler. I shake my head and laugh as we climb on the bus. He and I find seats together and once we sit down he slinks even lower to reach into his pockets. In one hand he pulls a deck of cards. In the other out a flask.

"Care for a wee tipple" he says in a really bad Scottish accent while giving the flask a little shake.

"Yeah why the hell not." I take a sip and immediately cough so hard I almost spit it up. "What the hell is that!?"

"Coconut rum. Liz had the same damn reaction. It tastes like vacation and I won't apologize for it." He says as he takes back the flack in frustration.

"I just needed a heads up is all. You go in with the Scottish accent so I'm expecting, you know, Scotch."

"Oh, ha, yeah that was misleading. Welp, now you know it's coconut rum and we're going to play Gin Rummy."

I take another sip of the coconut rum and spot Nora running to the bus. She must have gotten out of her meetings early because she was going to take the later bus. She climbs aboard and slides into the seat in front of Chandler and me. She kneels on the seat and rests her arms on the back of the chair facing us.

"If anyone asks, I was totally sick all weekend, got it? That meeting was running long so I faked a headache and ran here." She eyes the flask. "Ooo, gimme gimme."

Chandler and I watch her for a reaction to the coconut rum.

"What?" She asks before taking a sip. "Is it like not booze or something?"

"No, it's booze," I say.

"Thought so," she takes a sip. "MMmm coconut rum is a fun choice!" Nora says unphased and tosses back another. She hands the flask back and settles into her seat.

"You excited to see Adam again Nora?" Chandler asks while shimmying his shoulders.

She turns again in her seat and looks at us.

"Eh, sure. Although, I think he was actually into Liz last time. If she hadn't passed out on the sofa it might have gone differently. And, nothing against your brother, but I don't really do repeats." She looks out the window as she finishes and then turns her attention to me. "So Kyle, now that you're single and ready to mingle, are you excited for this weekend away?"

"I guess so, I'm mostly excited about sleeping in, running on the beach, and seeing all the stars. I'm ready for a break from the city."

"Ugh you're such an old man. Please tell me you're going to party too." Chandler says.

I grip him on the shoulder and reassure him. "Yes man, I will party too. Now deal the cards."

"You're gonna be in here again Nora. And we'll have Liz in here too. Since she's last I think you should totally make her take the top bunk but I'll leave that up to you two to decide." Chandler is standing in the hallway outside our bedroom which has two sets of bunk beds in it.

I hadn't given much thought to the sleeping arrangements and I'm both excited and annoyed to be sharing with Liz and Nora. At least Liz won't be here until tomorrow so I won't have to worry about how I'm acting around her tonight.

There is no denying that I like her. That I crave her laughter. I look forward to seeing her in the morning when I get into work. I don't want to rush into anything but I can clearly envision dating her, holding her hand. Doing everyday things with her will make them more special and doing the special things in life with her will make them unforgettable.

I think I'm falling for her. Hard.

After settling in a bit Chandler and Adam got things started at the pool with a cannonball contest. Things quickly evolved from there as the drinks kept flowing and now they're picking songs for everyone's "walk off" where you have to walk straight into the pool like you don't know it's there. I'm having a lot more fun than I expected.

I also learned that Chandler's cousin, Fiona, is a teacher and her friend Amie works at an afterschool program that goes into schools to coordinate STEAM activities. We're sitting on neighboring pool loungers and I am getting so many ideas for the summer camp. Her students experience the drop off of attendance and performance over the summer too. I've had a few beers so I won't be forgetting much but I want to write these ideas down anyways.

I stand and tell Amie that I'm headed inside to grab my notebook. I start walking and when I look up Liz is standing with her bag in the kitchen watching me through the patio doors. I come to a stop when our eyes connect because I am shocked to see her. Something sad flashes through her eyes before she recovers, smiles, and waves.

"Hey Kyle. Umm, surprise." She says with a shrug when I get through the door.

"Hi Liz! You're here? I didn't think you were coming until tomorrow."

"My parents were bored with my big city life so I drove out here."

"How could they have been bored? Didn't you have art tours and shows lined up?" I take her bag from her and start to walk towards our room.

"Oh, Thanks. And, yeah we did. But those only ate up like two hours and by four this afternoon we were just sitting and looking at each other at a coffee shop. We'd already been over the Brooklyn Bridge, through shops, to an immersive show, and we had run out of things to talk about."

I set her bag down on the bed. I had decided to take the top bunk so one of the larger beds below is still available. "Thanks," she says while tucking her hair behind her ear.

I can tell something is going through her head. She looks uncomfortable. Or maybe she's tired. She did just drive out here from the city in rush hour traffic. I don't want to pressure her into a conversation so I'm going to share my news and let her have a moment alone.

"Well I'm glad you're here early." I stick my hands in my pockets. "Get this, Fiona's friend, Amie, has some awesome ideas for the camp. She thinks some kids would probably come all summer and that we should do some sort of 4-H program that they can work towards." I reach into my bag looking for my notebook and pen and continue while I search. "Then each week could have a theme so the kids can sign up based on interest. A family camp would be incredible but there are challenges with parents and caregivers getting time off."

I stand up straight with my notebook and pen and Liz is looking at me with a small smile on her face.

"Are you coming out back?" I ask.

"Nah, I'm pretty tired, I might actually just read in bed."

"Oh, okay. Well, I'm excited to hang out tomorrow. Chandler said we're going down to the beach. Apparently Brando and Carolina are packing up coolers for us to take."

"Sounds fun."

"Okay, well," I pause at the door and turn back towards her. Liz is standing next to her bed with her arms crossed, shoulders slumped in, and her head turned down towards the floor. She seems subdued. Small. I hate seeing her with this body language. I wish I knew her better so I could help navigate whatever she's feeling. Talk through whatever is bringing her down.

Ever since Chandler announced this weekend getaway and Liz said yes I've been picturing spending the day with her on the beach. Playing games, reading on a towel, swimming. Liz in a bikini.

Maybe she's just tired and hopefully with some rest she'll be more like her usual self tomorrow.

"See you later then." I say with a knock of my knuckles on the doorframe.

"See ya."

And with that I leave the room and head back out to the pool loungers.

CHAPTER 21

LIZ

After seeing Kyle chatting up a beautiful girl when I first walked into the house I wasn't in the mood to party so I took a shower, got into my PJs, and read my romance novel in bed. This one has a one bed on a business trip scenario which is sort of ironic because Kyle and I are sharing a room.

Yes, it's also with Nora.

And there are technically four beds.

But still.

He's on the top bunk on the other side of the room, above Nora, who didn't settle in until 2am. Kyle came in around midnight. I pretended to sleep. Once I stopped obsessing over whether he was asleep yet or not, I fell asleep too. Eventually.

So while I went to bed early, I didn't get much sleep. And I woke up early this morning which is so not my M.O. but the idea of laying here until Kyle or Nora wakes up has me itching with anxiety so I get out of bed as quietly as I can and head to the main area of the house.

Carolina is in the kitchen, she has a pot of coffee already brewed and is putting together quiches for us. A girl could get used to this.

I take a cup of coffee and my laptop out with me to the patio. When I decided to head out here last night my parents and I got a cab back to my apartment. They decided to stay the rest of the weekend and loan me their car for the drive. I packed up as quickly as I could, and remembering how I only wore swimsuits last time, I had room for more photography props. I can take some stock photos and get them uploaded quickly for people to use before summer ends. Things like a rattan bag, extra sunglasses, sunscreen, hair accessories, a frisbee. I'll use other stuff that Chandler has. I bet I can get people to be hand models too because the images with hands always sell.

The morning is already warm and I can tell it is going to be a beautiful beach day. A few of the shots I got last week need editing so I open my laptop and pull them up. I hear the patio door slide open behind me and Kyle steps out in blue PJ pants, a plain but well worn gray t-shirt, and his hair is mussed in an adorable way.

"Mornin'," he manages with a nod.

"Morning," I reply.

"You're up early. I didn't take you for a morning person." Kyle says as he crosses over the patio and leans against a post.

"I'm an inconsistent morning person. I can rise and shine and stay in bed all day with the best of them. How about you, are you a morning person?"

"Always have been. When I was a kid I'd wake up at like 5:30 and build with LEGOs until my parents woke up and made us breakfast. Then eventually I learned how to pour my own cereal." He takes a sip of his coffee and I watch his adams apple work while he swallows and am surprised to find it alluring. "What are you doing there?" He nods towards my laptop.

"I took some photos this past week. I'm having a look at them. Might do some editing."

"Can I see?"

"Sure." I pause for a moment, unsure if he's going to get up and come to me or if he's waiting for me to just turn my laptop around. I'd be lying if I said I didn't want him to come over here. For a chance to be close to him. And as if the Universe hears me, he pushes off the post he was leaning on and walks my way. He stands behind the chair, reaches his arm over to set his coffee down and leans on the table, his other arm on the back of the chair. I'm surrounded by him.

I open up the first photo. It's of people stepping into a crosswalk. There's a woman's feet with heels on, a man's feet with loafers, and another man's feet with slip on sneakers. That guy's skateboard is also in view. I tried to get a picture of him starting on his board but I didn't want to stop and squat in the middle of the street to capture it.

"Oh cool."

I exhale without realizing I was holding my breath. I move to the next photo which is a close up of a woman pressing the walk button. All we see is her manicured hand with a bracelet. I want to get another one with a man's hand. Maybe another one with someone holding their coffee cup.

"Liz," Hearing my name in his voice this close to me does something to my stomach. It's like that feeling when you're about to crest the top of the roller coaster but way less terrifying. "These are great. I mean I've got nothing to compare them to and know nothing about art but I feel like I could see these on a business's website."

"I know right? These ones are corporate but kinda fun."

He stands up and walks over to a chair at the end of the table. He takes a seat and faces out towards the yard. I wish I knew what was going on in his head. Does he think this photography is a waste of time? I'm definitely not going to tell him I was late to work because I stopped to take these. How lame does that make me look? What do we talk about next? Do I just go about editing my photos like he's not there? Did he sleep well last night? Or was it awkward for him too? Is he into that Amie girl? Is he into me?

I can't deny that I got a little riled up inside when he was standing so close. I don't know if he and Tiffany actually broke up after he said "I'm done" at the bar or if it was just a fight. He didn't say anything about it at work this week but the last time I asked him was on Monday. Maybe they got back together? What am I supposed to do with these I'm-about-to-drop-off-the-edge-of-the-world stomach vibes if I don't even know if he's available?

"So, can I ask what happened with you and Tiffany?"

He chokes on the coffee he was sipping. Whoops. I guess that was kind of out of nowhere if you haven't been privy to the conversation happening in my head.

"Ha yeah, you can." He sets his coffee on the table as he swivels his chair in my direction. His crystal clear blue eyes meet mine for a split second before he looks down at his hands he just clasped. "At the bar I accidentally read a text on her phone. He basically said he was still thinking about them together."

"Shit Kyle. That's horrible. I'm so sorry."

"You don't need to be sorry. It is what it is."

"Well, sure, but that's still terrible."

Oh man, I feel so bad for him. That sucks. I haven't been cheated on myself but I can imagine the pain.

But, also, hold the phone, Kyle is available.

Suddenly I'm very thankful that Tiffany cheated.

He brings his gaze up and is looking straight at me. I cannot read his expression. I hope mine isn't gleeful because even though that's what I'm feeling inside that shouldn't be the expression on my face.

"I broke it off, obviously."

"Yeah," I whisper and keep eye contact with him. This moment feels charged. There's something passing between us. He places his hand on the arm of his chair to start and stand up. I feel my breath catch.

"MORNING!" Nora slides the door open quickly and birds fly out of the nearby trees. "Who's ready to get drunk on the beach?!"

"Ha, good morning Nora," Kyle says as he stands up. He looks back at me over his shoulder as he walks into the house and his eye contact seems to say a lot but I'm not sure what.

Ouch.

I'm not a morning person today.

I crack on eye open and review everything I learned yesterday.

First, I learned that Kyle is not with Tiffany anymore.

Second, I learned that she cheated. What a capital B.

Third, I learned that Adam makes wicked strong drinks.

All day I thought I caught Kyle watching me. Or like handing me something I was about to reach for. He held props close as I took a few pictures. And I was so nervous. I don't think I realized the enormity of my crush on Kyle until he told me yesterday morning that he and Tiffany had broken up.

It was over Adam's margaritas and lawn games yesterday afternoon that I dwelled on the fact that all the attention this past week was from Single Kyle. He was so nice. He took serious interest in my photography and family and he actually encouraged me to take more photos.

More than nice. He had been kind.

And I'd been nice, and kind I hope, back.

It wasn't until yesterday that I started to feel awkward around him. I mean yeah, he is attractive and I got a little flustered around him at work at first but nothing serious. And probably nothing that's out of the ordinary.

So with all these thoughts going through my head on a loop I started feeling nervous around him. And nervous Liz turned into drinky Liz. And I don't really wanna think too hard about last night because one, my head is currently pounding and two, I'm sure I did something embarrassing.

At least he's not in bed next to me.

Although he's not in his bed either.

And it looks like I've been here alone all night. Allow me to arrange the supporting facts. I'm still fully dressed. Including my left flip flop. There is a smudge of makeup on my pillow that looks like a stamp of my face. And next to my pillow is a box of cheddar rabbit crackers.

I find the courage to roll to the side and muster the strength to get myself sitting up.

After that, I wait a few beats to get used to this new, upright position and then shuffle to the bathroom. I wash my face, slip on a giant sweatshirt over the dress I wore yesterday, and pad out to the kitchen. Kyle is already at the counter. Adam is passed out on the sofa and Kyle gives me the shhhh sign and nods towards the patio.

"How are you feeling today champ?" he chides, too loudly after he closes the sliding door.

"Shhhh, ow, not like a champ. Is there gatorade in the fridge?"

"Yeah, I'll grab you one." And with my head on my arms on the table and one eye open I watch him walk back inside.

CHAPTER 22

KYLE

I can't help but smile as I get a gatorade for Liz. Yesterday after everyone else woke up and got some breakfast we made our way out to the beach. Liz took some photos when we first got there and it was interesting to watch her process. She would organize objects, take a picture, check it, move something like an inch or swap it for something else and repeat. She packed up her camera after only thirty minutes and then we played volleyball, tossed the frisbee around, had chicken fights in the water, and drank, a lot. At one point last night, after several margaritas, I heard Liz saying to Nora "Why didn't you tell me he and Tiffany weren't together?!" I think she meant to whisper it but, tequila.

Then I watched as Liz had herself a little party. Dancing, singing, and suggesting a game of Catch Phrase which she dominated even being as drunk as she was.

She looks like she's in pain this morning.

I feel for her, we've all been there, but she also looks so dang cute.

"I was gonna hit the road early and get back to the city. When were you planning to leave today?" I ask as casually as I can as I hand her the gatorade. I'd love to drive her back to the city, even if she sleeps last night off the whole time. But I don't want her to know how badly I want that time with her, I'm still not totally sure how she feels.

"Uuugh, I dunno. I'm going to need a shower before I make any plans. I definitely don't want to drive home by myself."

I chuckle and catch her half smile. There's a pause, I wouldn't call it awkward. It's a silence we're both in as we both look out at the yard.

"It's really pretty here. Reminds me of home." Liz says with kind of a sigh.

"When's the last time you were home?"

"For a few weeks between school ending and the internship starting. I'll probably go back in a few weeks for Float Fest."

"That's the boat parade thing right?"

"Yeah and like town fundraiser carnival night. It's small town vibes and incredibly cheesy and I absolutely love it." Another pause. Her brown eyes are staring off into the distance. She shifts and turns towards me.

"Thanks for the gatorade. I'm gonna go shower. You wanna drive back to the city together?"

"Yeah, totally!" Calm down man, play it cool. "Okay. See you in a bit."

I can tell that the gatorade helped. She said the shower helped too. The diner-on-the-side-of-the-high-way pancakes and coffee helped the most.

We're almost to her apartment and I don't want to stop hanging out. How do I say 'can I come up?' without sounding like, ya know, I *wanna come up* with a winky face?

"Can you help me with my bag?" She offers as we turn onto her block. "My dad just texted that they're at The Met so I don't expect them for at least an hour."

YES! I almost yell. Great idea. Help bring the bag inside and then boom you'll be in the apartment! And you'll have some time with her before leaving and not having the 'meet the parents moment.'

"Yes actually, I'd love to. Oh look, a parking spot!"

"Thanks for carrying that bag up. It's mostly photo accessories since I learned last time that I'd be drinking in a swimsuit all weekend. I was way over packed for that one."

"Be Prepared as the Scouts say."

She lets out a little laugh. And then grabs the side of her head and groans.

"You had yourself a little party last night didn't you." I can't keep the affection from my voice.

"Tell me about it." she says as she crosses over to the kitchen to get water.

"Well, first you decided karok-"

She spins around and puts her hand over my mouth. "I didn't mean actually tell me about it." She giggles, pulls her hand away, and throws a friendly punch my way before taking a sip of water. "I want bagels."

"Let's get you bagels," I says with determination.

I'm now carrying bagels back to her apartment. She's eating it as she walks but we're only a block away and neither of us are finished. Am I going to come back up? Is she just going to give me a high five and say 'see you tomorrow buddy'? I know I don't want to be done hanging out with her today. But I've never made the first move with a girl I've gotten to know and like. It's been hookups first followed by maybe getting to know them better.

Tiffany was my longest, air quotes, relationship. And I wasn't super invested in it. Neither was she for that matter. But it also started with a hookup and then we continued to hang out.

With Liz I've been doing the getting to know you, hanging out stuff, and want to add in the intimate stuff. I'm borderline obsessed with it. I have had a hard time not fixating on her lips as she sucks from her iced coffee straw. It's no surprise I am envisioning her mouth around something else.

The bagel and coffee brings Liz to life. She's chatting about how she takes structural engineers for granted because they're the people that make everything and it's a miracle that we can all go about our days without buildings crashing down on us or roads buckling.

I'm learning she's a carbs after a night out girl. She got so excited for the pancakes at Ellen's Pancake Hut I thought she was going to cry.

She is fun to be around.

I like hanging out with her. Like, I *like it* like it.

Ugh, I sound like a middle schooler.

I'm lost in thought so I almost miss her question. "You wanna watch a movie? I usually spend a hungover afternoon watching a movie I've seen before so I can pass out and not miss anything."

"Let's do it. Have you seen Tommy Boy?"

"It's only one of the best movies ever made."

"I agree." And she starts to unlock her building's door when someone calls from the sidewalk behind us.

"Lizzard!"

I turn to see who it is and catch a whispered 'oh no' from Liz.

"Mom! Dad, hi." She says with a big smile and a nervous lit to her voice. She flicks her gaze up to me quickly but I don't think there's time for us to get out of this.

"Who's your friend?" Her mom says from halfway down the block while kind of wiggling her eyebrows. If Liz got her social skills from her mom we're in for trouble.

"Mom, Dad, this is Kyle Sutherland. He's my fellow intern at Fosters. Kyle, my Mom and Dad."

"Nice to meet you." I say as I reach my hand out to shake, first her mom then her dad.

"Well, c'mon up and get the car keys and then you can go." Liz says as she walks into the vestibule of her building leaving me holding the door.

"What's the rush Lizzard? We want to hear all about your weekend with your friends?" Her mom says as she climbs the stairs behind Liz.

"The usual, drinking at the beach, drinking at the pool." Liz trails off as she opens her apartment door.

"Well that sounds like so much fun." Her mom replies.

I'm following her dad up the stairs, from what Liz has told me he's the one who has discouraged her photography career. I am tempted to call him on it. To say that she also took photos this weekend and that they're selling and that she is building a name for herself but I literally just met these people. I want to defend Liz, support her, not make things more difficult by stirring the pot.

"Still taking those photos I see." Her dad says as he eyes the camera on the counter.

"Yep. I got some good ones at the beach yesterday." Liz says quickly, and quietly.

"It was fun to watch her work." I say, hopefully Liz sees it as a supportive comment, not an antagonizing one. But her dad has turned around to look at me now with a keen interest in his eye.

"And, Kyle was it?" I nod. "What are your plans after this internship is over?"

"Well sir, my aunt is the president of YouthFull, an afterschool program foundation in the Bronx. I'll be working there establishing a summer camp program for their students."

"That's wonderful!" Liz's mom exclaims quickly, obviously an effort to cut off her husband and make sure he doesn't have any follow up questions. "Now, Kyle dear, where are you from?"

"Outside of Waterbury, Connecticut."

"Lovely, and where did you go to school?"

"Yale, ma'am."

"Impressive. And you're going into non profits?" Her dad asks. I can see Liz over his shoulder leaning against her bedroom door. She mouths "sorry" to me but I just smile. This is nothing.

"That's the plan. I earned a Humanities degree focused on Urban Studies; how the structure of our cities impacts human behavior. Then I went right into a two year joint MBA and MPH program."

I catch Liz's eye and smirk. She knew I went to Yale but we never really talked about what degrees I earned. I think she assumed I got a management degree, or a pre-law degree like Jeff. We also haven't talked about the fact that I'm two years older than she is.

"Well son, that's very impressive." Liz's dad says and then he looks over at his wife. She is busy looking between Liz and I. "Katherine, let's pack up and head home. Give these kids some space."

"Oh sure, of course." Katherine says as she makes her way to Liz's bedroom. She passes Liz and gives her a hug while Liz keeps her eyes trained on me. I offer up a little shrug and a smug smile because she's told me what's important to her dad. The best education money can buy. And I happen to have one of those. Well, technically three of them.

CHAPTER 23

LIZ

Kyle is on my couch.

Kyle is two years older than me.

Kyle has not one, not two, but three degrees from Yale.

Kyle met my parents today.

Kyle *impressed* my parents today.

Kyle is sitting next to me on my couch.

My head is spinning.

Half from the left over booze, half from the fact that Mr. Yale Graduate Kyle McShoulders is on my couch.

We're laughing at Tommy Boy. He is quoting lines without realizing he's doing it. It's super cute. And tough to reconcile with the whole, three degrees from Yale thing.

And he smells good. I know because I'm sitting a little too close with my legs tucked up under me so I'm forced to lean even closer.

He seems to be leaning closer too.

The credits start to roll and I officially feel disappointed that he never made a move. I shift and start to stand when Kyle reaches out and grabs my wrist.

I'm not sure he even realizes that he has until we both go from looking at his hand on my arm to each other. He gently tugs my arm and I slowly sit down with my legs tucked under me again. We stare at each other for what feels like eternity.

He reached out and gently touches my chin. I drop my gaze to his mouth, to his lips that are full but firm and when I look back up into his eyes I realize he's looking at my lips too. I maintain eye contact because if I close my eyes I'm not sure I'll believe this is real.

He gently pulls my chin towards him and in a flash of electricity his lips are on mine.

Is it possible to feel weak in the knees when you're sitting down?

Yes.

Yes it is.

This kiss is unlike any other. It's firm and powerful but soft and tender. He's starting slow. His fingers are a whisper of a touch under my chin. I want to stay here with our lips pressed gently together forever.

His tongue slowly pushes against my lips and I inhale as I tilt my head and open my mouth to him. His hand slides from my jaw, grazes down my neck, and then his fingers comb into the hair at the back of my neck. Tingling sensation runs down my spine and my breath catches.

He pulls back, still holding my head in his hand, and looks at me with concern.

"You okay?" He sounds as breathless as I feel.

"Yeah, very okay," I smile and this time I lean in to kiss him. His arm that was on the back of the sofa wraps around my low back and his other stays at the nape of my neck. My hands hold onto his shoulders for dear life.

Suddenly, or maybe it is several hours later I'm not sure, he pulls away and moves his hands down my arms. He rests his forehead on mine. I let out a sigh.

"Wow." He whispers. I shrug and smile at Kyle and he smiles in return but asks, "What's the shrug for?"

"I'm sorry, I just, I don't know what you want or what we're doing or if this is a good idea or-"

"Liz, it's fine. We're good. We don't have to figure anything out tonight."

"Okay," is all I can say with a sheepish smile.

"I had a lot of fun hanging out today. A lot of fun this weekend with you. I'm going to get going now because I don't want to get carried away or do anything too quickly. Have a good rest of your night. I'll see you tomorrow." He says all of this as he stands and moves to my door.

"Okay." I say as I lean on the back of my sofa looking at him. "See you tomorrow."

CHAPTER 24

LIZ

To say I'm a ball of nervous energy at the office this morning is an understatement.

I am a side-of-the-highway World's Largest ball of nervous energy.

C'mon folks! Step right up! Watch as the one, the only, Liz Collins of Lakeville, NY as she attempts to break the world record for tamping down her anxiety because she made out with her coworker last night.

There's no doubt in my mind that it was meant to happen. Kyle was made for kissing. I could feel the path his hands took long after I got into bed last night.

He texted me when he got home to ask if I wanted to come over tonight after work for dinner. I also texted Nora last night to tell her that Kyle and I kissed. Right now that's feeling like a bad decision because she's bouncing her eye contact between us.

"Can you stop that?" I hiss at her.

"Stop what?"

"Looking at me, us, like that." I say while quickly motioning between Kyle and I with my finger hoping I've kept the gesture behind my laptop screen.

"I'm just excited for you! I want to know all the details. How long has this been a thing?" She's not even whispering anymore and I sheepishly look at Kyle who is grinning at me. Great. Cat's out of the bag.

"Nora, can you not? It's not a *thing*, it was a kiss."

"But you said it was the best kiss you've ever had?" She looks genuinely hurt that I don't want to discuss this.

At work.

In front of Kyle.

"You said that?" Kyle asks.

"Said what?" Chander asks as he walks into the conference room.

Fan-freaking-tastic. How do I change the subject? How do I get Judy in here to disturb the peace? Create some sort of filing disaster that means we all have to be in separate rooms for the rest of the day and no one does anymore talking about this.

"Liz and I kissed yesterday." Kyle says to Chandler. I can feel my eyes bugging out of my head as I look at him. "And she told Nora it was the best kiss she's ever had."

I gasp and throw my pen at him. He annoyingly catches it and I hear Chandler and Nora laughing.

"I can't believe you—" I start and don't finish because Judy walks in.

The rest of our day goes by quickly between note taking, proofreading, researching, and stapling. I went home after work and swapped jean shorts for the khaki pencil skirt I wore to the office. I am now standing outside Kyle's door. I can smell food being cooked on the other side, and I'm already impressed before he even lets me in.

"Hey!" He says as he opens the door. "Make yourself at home."

"Don't mind if I do" I say as I slip off my sandals and leave them by the door. Last time I was here I was too overwhelmed by his proximity to my knees that I barely noticed what his place looked like. The studio apartment is tidy and decorated in grays and blues. There are some sports posters on the walls but not a lot of books or knick knacks. His bed is made. His closet doors are closed. There are throw pillows on the sofa. The kitchen counter is bare except for the food he's preparing, which looks to be chicken, vegetables, and something cooking in a pot on the stove.

I make the full spin back around to where he's standing at the counter and he's smiling at me. I smile back. I'm nervous but not terribly so. The right amount of nervous. The level that tells me this is a good thing.

"So—"

"So." We both say at the same time. Then I laugh and he laughs. He recovers more quickly.

"Want some sparkling water to drink?"

"Yes please." He walks over to the fridge and hands me a can. "Thanks." I say as I take the can from him. "I really like your apartment. How did you find one on such short notice? I was scrambling in the three weeks we had between hearing about the internship and it starting."

"My cousin, Bryan, actually had it before me. He just moved down to DC for work so he is subletting it to me."

"He's the performance coach right?"

"Yeah, he does executive coaching for sports professionals."

"That sounds made up." I say with a smile.

He chuckles. "It kind of is. He created his own job. He was a physical therapy major in college and when he got out he started working as a trainer for the New York Rovers hockey team. One of the marketing guys was in the weight room talking to a player when he overheard Bryan giving advice on how to mentally bounce back from a bad shift. This marketing guy pulled him aside and asked if he was a sports psychologist and Bryan kind of laughed. He told him he was a trainer with a good head on his shoulders. A few weeks later he got an email from the marketing guy asking if he'd be a sounding board for some ideas before he presented them to his boss. Bryan said yes and they went out for beers.

"About a year later this marketing guy was promoted to be an assistant general manager. He and Bryan had been meeting and talking shop a lot. This guy basically told Bryan he was going to pay him to be his executive coach. Then word got around and other guys started asking for his help so he became this like consultant for a lot of the front office guys."

He turns to light the stove and begin cooking.

"This first marketing turned assistant GM guy got a job with the DC Wolves and he asked if Bryan would join him. So Bry moved down to DC, is working for this guy and has a few other clients. He's taking some classes at Georgetown to learn more but I think it's pretty cool that he's created this job for himself."

"That is really cool. And proves that good things happen when you say yes to opportunities."

"True. I'm certainly glad I said yes to the Fosters internship."

I smile because I'm pretty sure he's talking about me, not how he has learned how to fax documents.

"Did you have a lot of options?"

"Kinda." He says it with a shrug. Yesterday was the first day I found out about his educational acumen. Does he know how desperate I am for the Fosters job so he's trying to downplay his accomplishments? Did he have options? I only had one.

"The only other offer I had was with a company that sells software to construction companies. The job would be going around doing software demos and helping get things set up if they bought the products."

"Why didn't you do anything with photography?"

"Because photography isn't a job."

"Yes it is. You make money selling your photos."

"Yeah but it's not like a *career.*"

"What do you mean?" He genuinely asks.

"Like, if someone asks what I do I can't say I'm a 'stock photographer' no one knows what that is."

"No one knows what an 'Executive Coach for Sport Professionals' is either and Bryan has made it work."

"I guess." I reply with a shrug. He's seriously going to make this about me and my photography and I'm sure he saw how my dad lit up with all the Yale talk yesterday. Brown is technically an Ivy League school but when your siblings go to Harvard and Dartmouth it pales in comparison.

"Plus with everyone needing photography and video for their social media I bet you could get a lot of work doing photoshoots for brands or individuals. Like headshots and stuff."

"Yeah, probably."

"Why don't you sound excited about this?"

"Ugh, I dunno Kyle. It's just not what I want to do I guess. Like I want to have a job at Fosters where I can help people. Where I can make a difference."

That, and I'm scared.

Terrified.

Of failure.

Of not being as impressive as my siblings.

Of not doing *enough.*

"I don't know if Fosters is the place to *make a difference.*" He says with a scrunched up nose as he puts the chicken in the pan.

"Well I don't have an Aunt who has a foundation with a job created just for me." And I regret saying it as soon as it comes out of my mouth. "Sorry, I didn't mean that."

"No, it's cool. I get it. Sometimes I forget that the Fosters internship is more important to you guys than it is to me. I just think that your photography is good, it seems to make you happy, and you could make it a career if you wanted to."

"Okay, sure, I'll think about it."

"Okay, sure." He says as he turns back around and adds the vegetables to the pan.

"Can we talk about something else?" I ask, looking down and picking at my manicure.

"Of course, what do you think of the invite to the workshop this week?"

When Judy came in and interrupted our conversation this morning, albeit a few moments too late to save me from humiliation, she did so to tell us about a Fosters workshop that was happening this week. On Thursday all the consultants and partners are coming into town for meetings and presentations. The meetings are all day Thursday and Friday and on Friday night there is a reception. Actually, they call it a "Gala". Knowing that I dressed poorly for the first event of the summer I am tempted to ask one of the partners what they're going to wear.

"I think I'm nervous about what to wear." I answer honestly.

Kyle laughs. "Again, another thing I take for granted. I can put on a suit and call it a day. Do you have the dress code printed on a poster at home?"

I laugh. "I should! I can't seem to get it quite right."

"I think you're fine. I think they're the ones who need to chill out."

"I agree with you but my wardrobe seems like the low hanging fruit. Like if I can get what I'm wearing right then they can focus on my work instead of my appearance."

"Fair enough. I wish I could help you but I've got nothing to offer when it comes to fashion advice."

"No, it's fine. I'll ask Nora and maybe Lauren can help."

"I heard that she and Marcus are an item."

"What? Really? From who?"

"Deb mentioned something off hand when I was helping her get a box down from storage. She was asking if I liked working with Lauren and Marcus and I said that I did and she said 'not as much as they like working with each other' and when I looked at her she smiled, took the box, and walked away."

"Ohmigosh! Deb is such a gossip! I would LOVE to just sit at her desk all day and gab."

"She certainly knows a lot of the happenings around the office." He turns off the burner. "Alright. Chicken stir fry is done. You good if I pile things up in a bowl for you?"

"That sounds great."

CHAPTER 25

KYLE

"This would be such a cute spot to photograph."

"Bring your camera next time." I love that there will be a next time. I am feeling beyond happy with Liz in my apartment, sharing a meal with her on the landing of my fire escape, enjoying the ebb and flow of our conversations.

So far I have learned that her favorite color is green. Any green. She's learned that mine is blue, like the ocean. Growing up we both played soccer and basketball. She played tennis in high school and I played hockey. I've learned she hates tomatoes, loves pancakes (which I already knew), and that her favorite dessert is creme brûlée.

"If creme brûlée isn't an option then I'll go for anything with fruit and hopefully, if the restaurant is doing it right, they'll add a scoop of ice cream to the baked dessert. That's really the only way to eat something like pie or cobbler."

"You're so right. Wanna go get ice cream now?"

"Umm, sure."

I laugh, "no pressure, we don't have to."

"No, yeah, I want to go, I just wasn't expecting it that's all." She sounds excited but also a little distracted.

"I like to keep you on your toes." Because her genuine smile, like the one she's sharing with me now, is the most beautiful thing I've ever seen. Her practiced, professional smile is lovely too but this is spectacular.

"C'mon, there's a Gelateria a few blocks east."

"Yum! I love gelato."

"Especially in the summer, it hits the spot."

She brings her dishes to the sink, rinses them, and then dries her hands on the towel hanging off the oven handle. It's such a small, everyday moment but watching it, watching her from where I'm standing just inside the window of my fire escape, sends a flurry of butterflies through my stomach.

She turns around and smiles at me and wipes her hands on her shorts.

"I'll just grab my bag and we can go." She says with a shrug.

"Sounds good."

I rinse my dish, stack it on hers and then meet her at the door.

"What's your go to flavor?"

"Oh that's a tough one. If they know what they're doing the classic stracciatella is fantastic. But so is lemon. And pistachio. And I read a book once where the character ate some that was pine nut flavored and she said it was delicious."

"Ha, so any of them are your favorite."

"Pretty much." She says with a shrug.

"I go with chocolate, every time."

"You know what you like huh."

"Yeah I do." I say while looking at her. She senses my gaze as she walks past me out the lobby door and looks up at me. I hope she understands that I meant it. I know I like her. I wasn't subtle. I am determined to take this slowly. It's why I stopped us from getting physical last night. My body was screaming for me to continue with her. To continue to taste her, feel her. Even now, just thinking about kissing her has my blood pumping faster.

She breaks eye contact and looks back down the sidewalk in front of her. I hold my hand out, slightly, and when she slips her hand in mine and our fingers intertwine I am reassured that taking it slow will be worth it. The gelato shop is just another block away. I find my thumb has started to circle against the back of her hand as we walk.

I could walk like this forever.

I might try.

We reach the shop and I hold open the door for her. When she walks past me she tries to pull her hand away but I grip it tighter and end up moving my arm up and over her head. Our fingers twirl just right so now I have my arm around her shoulder but I'm still holding her hand. Liz's back is pulled up against my chest and I rest my chin against the side of her head.

Together we look at the flavor options. After a few samples Liz picks stracciatella in a sugar cone and I order my chocolate in a dish. I regret that I do have to stop holding her in order to pay. She grabs a few napkins and waits for me by the door.

We step outside together and start walking back towards my apartment. We didn't talk about her coming back with me and as much as I am mesmerized by her tongue that keeps poking out to lick her cone, I will not be taking her back upstairs. I meant it when I said I wanted to take it slow and if she comes back upstairs I won't be able to restrain myself.

Liz is telling me about one of the best doppelgangers she's ever come across. A woman with curly, shoulder length hair was wearing a black hat with the word Paris embroidered across it and walking a pair of black poodles. She is chuckling to herself at the memory when some ice cream drips onto her t-shirt.

"What a fucking idiot." She mutters to herself as she scrambles for a napkin.

Is she calling the ice cream an idiot? Or herself?

She can't be calling herself an idiot for dripping ice cream on her shirt in the middle of July.

She lets out this little tisk sound that makes me think she is calling herself an idiot. Why would she do that? Over such a mundane thing that everyone does at one point or another.

I nudge her with my elbow. "Hey, it's no big deal." She is still trying to dab away at the spot.

"Ugh, I know, but like, c'mon Liz. Why can't I do anything right?"

Does she know how crazy she sounds?

"C'mon just finish your ice cream." I'm not sure what else to say to her.

"Yeah. Well if I was smart I would have gotten a dish like you."

"I didn't get a dish because I'm smart. I got one because I get annoyed having to eat the cone all by itself at the end. Those little sugar cones don't actually hold anything. The gelato just sits on top."

"Until it falls on your shirt." She says, I look over at her and I see her head bowed forward, shoulders slumped. How can I make this better?

Oh, I know.

I take a big scoop of my gelato, almost everything left in the cup. I slowly move it up to my mouth, turn to look at Liz and when I'm about half an inch away I turn the spoon and drop it.

The chunk of chocolate gelato lands on my chest and rolls down my shirt before landing on my shoe.

I couldn't have planned that any better.

I got to watch Liz watch the gelato. Her eyes doubled in size when it landed on my shoe. She flicks her eyes back up to meet mine.

I grin.

She grins.

But then she fights the smile and turns it into a scowl.

"Oh c'mon! You were smiling. Don't try to hide it."

"I hate you." But she totally doesn't. I tap my toe on the sidewalk to knock the gelato off of it and then scoop up the little that's left in my cup and eat it through a grin.

She's grinning too.

Half a block later we're standing outside my building. I hold my arm up to hail the cab that's coming up the street. Liz looks over her shoulder and sees it.

"Are we going somewhere else?" She asks.

"Nope. But it's a school night, you need to get home." I say it with a smile as I reach out and pull a strand of her hair between my fingers. It's unbelievably soft. I let the hair fall back to her shoulder.

"Thanks for coming over tonight Liz." The cab is almost to us.

"Oh, yeah, sure, thanks for having me." The cab pulls up and stops.

"I'll see you tomorrow." I reach and open the door for her. She pivots towards it but I stop her by gripping her upper arm. I pull her back up towards me and I lower my head towards her.

She tilts her head up and in one move I slide my hand up from her arm to her jaw and connect my lips to hers. She offers a sweet exhale as I deepen the kiss.

She tastes like vanilla and adrenaline. The combination sends a current of lust through me.

Because I am determined to take this slow, and I don't want the cabbie to start the meter on us, I pull back from the kiss and pivot to the front door. I open it, hand the guy a $20 and then go back to close the door for Liz.

"Bye Liz." I say as I lean down between the cab and the door.

"Bye Kyle." She replies, her eyes wide, her smile genuine.

I have fallen for her. Hard.

CHAPTER 26

LIZ

The person looking back at me in the mirror is me, for sure, I'd recognize that birthmark near my ear anywhere, but she's rocking a different vibe.

She's confident.

She's energetic.

She's had a grownup week.

Monday night was incredible. Gosh, it's five nights later and I still get a rush of giddiness when I think about it. First, Kyle cooked dinner for me. Then he took me out for ice cream. I know I messed up when I called myself an idiot out loud, usually that's just the voice in my own head. But then when Kyle purposely dropped a spoonful of chocolate ice cream on himself my system was flooded with joy. Without saying anything, without trying to tell me not to call myself an idiot, he moved past it and leveled the playing field.

And then, *then*, the kiss by the door of the cab. The door was freaking between us but it was maybe the best kiss of my life. It was pure romance.

Swoon.

I assumed we'd go back up to his place. I kind of wanted to. No, not kind of. I really wanted to. But now that I think about it he's been taking it slow all week and it is just building my anticipation for this weekend when we get to spend our time together.

Tuesday we didn't hang out but we texted a bit after work. I went to bed smiling, relaxed, and a little wound up about seeing him again the next morning.

Wednesday he walked me all the way back to my apartment after work and we ate falafel wraps from a street vendor on the way. Again, a quick kiss good night at my door.

Thursday we stayed late at work together after a full day of meetings at the workshop. Donald asked us to put together a booklet for his presentation today so we set up the old print and bind assembly line and got snacks from across the street. No kissing but lots of 'accidental' touches and heated looks.

Now it's Friday.

I'm not trying to put more pressure on him but like what does he have planned for tonight?

We're attending the Foster's Gala tonight and I feel like a bonafide grown up.

I got ready in an apartment that doesn't smell like pot. Thank you Nora.

I am wearing a forest green Grecian style dress with a low neckline, high leg slit, and praise cheeses, pockets.

I am wearing heels.

This event is to celebrate the firm's success over the past year. We've had two days of meetings and breakouts and I was so energized by it all. These people are out there doing the hard work of raising money every day. I learned so much.

I also learned that this employee gala is a big deal. Lauren called me into her office on Tuesday to discuss dress code and she actually pulled up a few dresses online as visual aids. They each cost what I expect two paychecks to be and on one hand I was annoyed that she was being so patronizing and on the other I really appreciated it.

Nora got the same talk from her managing partner, Trish. That night we went shopping at the department store last season discount shop and found our outfits and decided that we'd get ready together. So she's by my side as a colleague who is quickly becoming a friend. She's also my emotional support animal because there's no way I could have gotten myself to this point on my own. We're standing on the steps of Penn Station and we look good if I say so myself.

As we walk into the main room that is decked out in cocktail tables and golden up lighting against the wall, I realize that Lauren neglected to tell me something really important when she pulled me in for how-to-be-a-classy-lady 101.

That 'black tie optional' meant men in tuxes.

Specifically Marcus. In a tux.

Holy ovaries.

Yes I've been kissing, groping, and hanging out with Kyle all week and we're sort of an item I guess but I can objectively say that Marcus is a hottie with a body. I'd been working with him more closely in the last few weeks. Including a few late night email exchanges. And, I probably should have mentioned them to Kyle since we're meant to be working on the Sanderson Labs funding solutions together, and during the day we do, but I need the job from Fosters and Kyle doesn't so getting assignments straight from Marcus feels like an advantage.

Out of nowhere a waiter with champagne walks by and Nora and I each grab a glass. We clink them together and as I bring mine to my lips I say "What would HR think of me yelling that I'd like to personally be the one to relieve Marcus of those pants later?"

I am rewarded when Nora laughs down her first sip and almost has to spit it out.

"I think Patricia would have a small heart attack. She clutches those pearls tight. Although, I heard a rumor that he was dating a consultant last year before she left Fosters."

"Really? Interesting. I heard he and Lauren were hooking up."

"Should you be oogling your boss?"

"I'm not oogling, I'm noticing."

"Let me guess, you watch football for the pants right?"

"Doesn't everyone?"

Again, Nora laughs and rolls her eyes. I scan the crowd looking for Kyle and Chandler, and also trying to avoid staring at Marcus, when he catches my eye across the room. Marcus gives me a nod and lifts his champagne flute in my direction. I reciprocate and try to hide my grin by taking a sip.

Nora is saying something about taking a train to a Yale football game and I'm about to ask her to repeat it when Marcus appears at my side and his fingers brush the inside of my elbow.

"There are a few people I'd like you to meet Liz. Mind if I borrow her for a bit?" He leans over me and asks Nora.

She can't hide her eyebrows as they jump up her forehead but she says "Of course Marcus. She's all yours."

I glare at her as his grip on my elbow tightens and he turns me towards the center of the room. She can think he's a pompous ass but she has to agree that he's an attractive pompous ass. And he has an attractive ass.

Marcus sets his empty glass on a tray and replaces it and then does the same with mine. It was only then that I realized my glass was empty. I better find some water or I'm going to be flat out on my ass before long.

Marcus stayed at my side almost all evening. He introduced me to a few colleagues in different divisions and he got in a few good words for me with James Foster and his wife Mitsy.

I've never met a wife named Mitsy. Dog? Yes. I wonder what her given name is. Or maybe it says 'Mitsy' on her birth certificate. She comes from a long line of Mitsy St. Clairs and she is doing her mother proud. Or if it isn't her real name then at what point did she decide to change it?

Did she sit down with her bridge club and say, "Okay girls, today is the day, from now on I'm no longer Rebecca, I am Mitsy."

Does James call her Mitsy?

Like in the middle of love making is he panting out "yes, Mitsy, oh yes, Mitsy!"?

Gross.

Wait, is it short for Margaret? Mary Beth? Millicent?

If my name was Millicent I would definitely go by Mitsy as soon as possible.

But wouldn't Milly be a better nick name?

Marcus catches me daydreaming. He ducks a bit to meet my eyes and smiles. I return the favor and try to discreetly take a deep breath to help slow the blush I can feel creeping up my neck.

He glances at his, expensive I notice, watch and looks me in the eye. "Wanna head out soon? I've got a friend debuting a few pieces at a gallery opening tonight and told him I'd stop by after this."

"Oh, sure, umm, I'd love to."

"It's a date."

Wait. What?

"Ha yeah, I guess so. Will you excuse me? I'll meet you over by the door after a trip to the ladies."

I pivot as fast as I can towards the bathroom.

The girl I see in the mirror is not who I was expecting. I mean, it's me but she's smiling and her hair and makeup look really good. She's still the most adult version of me I've ever seen. And she just got asked out to a gallery opening by her boss, who just happens to be an uncomfortably attractive man.

Like, he's so pretty it's painful. And, UGH! He's nice. He spoke well of me to James and has been attentive all night. He laughed when I made a mistake over the location of someone's second home and gently corrected me. He asked me open ended questions and listened while I responded.

And now the invite to the party? Is this a test? Am I willing to go with the flow? Am I a team player? This could be my chance to really make an impression on one of the people responsible for hiring at Fosters.

The interns had talked about going out after the Gala. I'm sure they'll still go and I can meet them after the party. I owe it to Kyle to tell him about Marcus's invite. Technically we're on the same team and competing for the same position but he doesn't even want the job. So if this is a test of the employee compatibility system then I need to pass it if I want a chance.

And, yes, we're seeing each other I guess. So it might look back to someone on the outside that I left a party with another man. But it's not like that. This is for work. And I need this job. He'll understand.

I sling my clutch onto the counter and grab my phone.

LIZ: Hey! Marcus has been introducing me to everyone tonight. I think it's a good sign.

KYLE: Yeah I noticed.

LIZ: He just asked me to go to a party his friend is hosting. I feel like I should go, I don't want to give him any reasons to dislike me.

KYLE: Just you?

LIZ: Yeah

KYLE: Seems a little above and beyond but if you want to go then go.

LIZ: Ok

LIZ: Talk to you later

I tuck my phone back in my purse, reapply my lipstick, and as I walk out of the bathroom door I look up to see Marcus leaning on the banister. He smiles, holds his arm out for me, and we leave the party.

Nora and I had arrived in a taxi. Pooling our money because we both agreed that these dresses were too pretty for the subway.

Marcus has his own town car.

This is definitely the twilight zone because I'm in the back of a town car with a handsome man in a tux who is telling me about the artist we're going to see as he loosens his bowtie before taking it off. The artist is a 'boarding school buddy' and their families have homes in the Hamptons near each other.

Must be nice.

I attended suburban public schools my whole life. I won a photography contest and that helped get me into the arts program at Brown. Once there I earned my art minors and focused my majors on 'real job' subjects.

Brown does have an art scene so I'm not totally out of my depth heading to a gallery opening. I took plenty of art history classes and feel confident I can talk my way through this party.

We pull up and as the door opens I see flashing lights and the music is so loud I think I'm at a nightclub. I'm about to ask if it's the right place when Marcus leans down to take my hand and help me out of the car.

I feel like a dang princess.

There is a line around the corner and I take half a step in that direction as Marcus closes the door behind me. Then he marches right up to the cute girl at the door with the clipboard. I have to kind of skip to catch up since I was starting to walk the other direction. And skipping in heels is not recommended. I almost trip but manage to land against Marcus, holding my hands out and basically gripping his ass to keep me upright.

"Whoa! You alright?"

"Umm yep, no harm done. Thanks." I try to hide my embarrassment.

I look up and immediately recognize the cute girl in front of us. It's Tiffany.

The recognition hits her at the same time but she recovers faster than I do.

"OHMIGOSH Liz! Hi! How are you?!" and she reaches over for a hug and air kisses to each cheek. Marcus looks amused as he raises an eyebrow to me and all I can muster is a look of surprise.

How can she be so cheerful around me? Does she not know that I know she cheated? I mean, I was at the bar when Kyle read the text. I work with him every day. I've been kissing him. We're like basically dating! And I am really wishing I hadn't come out with Marcus tonight because I have no clue what to do now. I do know my protective instincts have fired up because I desperately want to show her Kyle is doing better without her.

I snap out of my thought process and manage "Tiffany! Hey! I'm so good. I'm excited to head in and see what this is all about."

"Oh yes. You'll love it. Listen, I'm on door duty for another 30 minutes but I'll come find you and we'll catch up!" And with that she motions to the door, smiles at Marcus, and turns her attention back to the person waiting in line.

CHAPTER 27

KYLE

Knock knock.

Thump.

"Shhhhhhit."

It's unlikely some random girl is trying to break into my apartment so I'm going to assume it is Liz.

I get up and open the door and sure enough.

She was leaning against the door when I opened it so she kind of trips but catches herself. She giggles as she closes the door and says "shhhhhh" to herself.

She's drunk.

She walks over to the kitchen to get a glass of water and leans on the island looking at her phone.

Her face is lit up in the glow of the screen and I can see that she's smiling. She's swaying a little bit. Her hair is still down and curling softly around her face. And her dress is as sexy as ever. I don't think she realizes how good she looked tonight. I watched her all night, from a distance because of that jerk Marcus, and she stood tall, proud, and charmed everyone around her.

"Have a fun night?" I ask.

Liz looks up at me and smiles. "I did, maybe too much fun." She lets out a puff of air from the side of her mouth. "I'm proud of myself for remembering where your apartment was."

I understand she went out to appease Marcus but I saw the way he was looking at her. Wolfish. He was just as drawn to her as I was. As I am. Did he touch her? Did he make a move? She's here which tells me no. But I'm just insecure enough to ask.

"Why did you come here instead of going home?" *Or back with Marcus?*

"Because I like liking you and I wanted to hang out and see you. I didn't get to hang out with you tonight."

"No you didn't."

"You're mad."

I smile. "I'm not mad."

"Don't do that, *I'm not mad, I'm disappointed,* thing." She adopted a baritone voice to imitate me.

I laugh. "That's not what I'm doing. I'm not mad, I'm not disappointed. I'm surprised. And I'm tired."

Her face sobers. "Oh no, were you asleep?"

"I was, but it's not a big deal. Wanna watch something?"

"Sure."

She makes her way across the room to my bed. Standing next to the dresser she reaches back and unhooks her bra, pulls it out of her dress, and drops it to the floor. I can never get her bra off that fast. Her nipples harden against the silk and I feel myself harden a degree too.

I have to physically try to slow my heart rate as she slides her dress down her body revealing a black g-string, steps out of it, and slides into my bed.

I'm fighting my reptilian brain. A really cute girl that I want to be in a relationship with is a little tipsy. No, she's drunk. She's in my bed, topless, in a g-string.

Chivalry might be dead but I am not.

Still, I won't make a move. I won't take advantage. I turn on the TV and I stay still until I know she's asleep then I head to the bathroom and take matters into my own hand.

It is no surprise that I wake up before Liz. She is sleeping on her side, with her hands tucked together under the pillow. The sheet has fallen down and I can see the top of her breasts between her arms. She's breathing lightly, the rise and fall of her chest being the only movement she makes. Her makeup is still on and smudged a little but in a soft way, not in a drunk girl crying at the end of the night way.

After taking a few more moments to soak her in I head to the kitchen to make coffee and put two frozen bagels in the toaster oven to thaw. I've made a little noise so she rolls over with a grunt and I smile at her from across the room.

"Oh good morning sunshine!" I say in my most chipper voice.

"Oww, c'mon Kyle. Not fair."

I whisper "Coffee is almost done and there's a bagel warming up."

"Have I told you lately that I love you?!" Her voice is hoarse.

My back is turned to her as she says this so she can't see my face but I'm sure she notices the way my head jerks up and my back stiffens. It's been a week and she's probably joking but the word love adds another layer to everything. I could see my feelings for her developing into the loving kind. Really easily. Who am I kidding, I'm already there. I think a part of me started falling for her back in April. I don't want to put it out on the line if she's just joking and quoting a silly old love song.

My head is in the fridge getting out the creamer so I don't hear her walk over to the kitchen. She stands right next to me and I almost toss the creamer in her face as I turn around. She laughs and takes a step back to grab her coffee. She found one of my tshirts to slip on but it just skims her bottom so I can see a hint of her backside when she turns around to take a seat at the counter.

"So I saw Tiffany last night."

"What? You did?" That is the last thing I expected her to say.

"Yeah she was working the door at the gallery opening Marcus took me to."

"Well that's fun." What am I supposed to say here? I'm battling some shock at not only hearing her name again but remembering that Liz was out with Marcus. "What a small world."

"Yeah it was weird. But the party was fun. Definitely the most trendy thing I've ever been to. Marcus went to boarding school with the artist and I put some of my art minor studies to use when I was talking with him. His friend picked up on my lingo and asked if I was an artist and, you'd be proud, I said I do some photography on the side."

"That's right you do. What'd he say?"

"He asked what kind and I nervously said stock photography. He said that was a really smart space to be in because people always need that type of visual support for their businesses. Basically what you told me."

"I won't say I told you so…."

She laughs and looks down at the counter. I see her take a breath. She looks up at me and her deep brown eyes lock with mine. "I haven't said it, but, thank you for your support with the photography stuff. Even if it's just talk for now. It means a lot."

I can tell that it took a lot for her to admit her gratitude out loud. It is important to me that she believes in herself. I've learned in the last few weeks that she needs encouragement in doses. Too much and she shuts down and I can't push her that far. I'm falling for this girl and her charm and talent and positive outlook.

"Do you have any plans today?"

"Well yesterday I would have said normal Saturday stuff. Groceries, laundry, photographs. But all of that can wait if it needs to. What are your plans today?"

"Normal Saturday stuff. Laundry, groceries, helping you take photographs, and then making you dinner."

She smiles and the toaster oven beeps. We enjoy our bagels together and everything feels right.

"THAT's how you fold shirts! How does it get so small?" I'm staring at Liz who is holding up a tiny rectangle that used to be my favorite Third Eye Blind t-shirt.

"It's the KonMarie method. I'll show you."

Liz walks me through a folding process that is remarkably simple and then miraculously stands my next t-shirt up on its side. She then explains how all the shirts will fit in the drawer more easily and will be 'standing at attention' when I need them.

"Amazing. How have I not heard of this?"

'I assume you don't spend your free time ogling well organized closets online.'

'No. That's not what I ogle online.'

Her adorable eye roll paired with a little laugh has me itching for more. I take the t-shirt out of her hand and drop it back on the pile before propping her up on the counter in the laundry room of my building. She's a little taller than me in this position on the counter and the angle of kissing up to her is incredible. This is how it should always be. Me looking up to her because, shit, she's amazing.

Her hands hold me in place on either side of my jaw and mine are on her thighs. She's wearing my t-shirt and a pair of gym shorts so I slide my hands down to her knees where the shorts end and slowly push up her thigh, dragging the fabric with me. I press my thumbs into her legs and she lets out the tiniest of whimpers as we kiss.

My mind is whirling with the sensation of her lips on mine. Their softness is welcoming, like I'm coming home to her. When I woke up this morning it felt like all was right with the world just because she was there sleeping next to me. We've only known each other a month but I feel so comfortable with her. So at ease. It is difficult to describe as anything besides serene.

Of course there's passion. There is no doubt in my mind I want all of her. I have to keep reminding myself to slow down because we're in the laundry room. I'm drawn to her like a magnet but the pull is more than physical attraction. It's an emotional attraction unlike anything I've ever felt before.

I want to support her. I want to build her up emotionally. I want to challenge her. Be there to celebrate wins and losses. Share life with her. I can't imagine doing laundry by myself ever again. Or coming home from work to spend the evening with anyone else. She just fits in my life. It feels comfortable.

CHAPTER 28

LIZ

Laundry should always be done while making out. Time passes so much more pleasantly. Kyle's kisses are almost lazy, like he could happily stay here all day. It feels like he's savoring me. I know I'm savoring him. In the last week I have experienced a wide array of Kyle Kisses and each stands tall on its own.

The first one? I'll never forget.

The cab door? Devastating.

The laundry counter? Exciting.

I was more than tipsy last night when I got to his place. I remember thinking about his arms around me while I was in the cab to his place. Then the feeling of being pressed against his chest in a hug. It didn't take long for my mind to wander to his hands running up my sides, then down to my lower back, and making their way up again to the nape of my neck.

I had to crack a window because I was feeling flushed.

When I woke up this morning to him in the kitchen making coffee I felt a pang of disappointment that we didn't hook up last night. It was quickly replaced by appreciation when I realized I stumbled into his apartment drunk and he simply tucked me in and went to sleep.

These moments, when he is thoughtful and patient, are the ones that have me feeling dizzy around him. When we first met there was a physical attraction, I mean look at the guy's shoulders. As we've gotten to know each other a deeper bond has developed. A friendship.

My heart goes all pitter-patter with the idea of *talking* with him. Of sharing my hopes and dreams. Yes my heart rate rises when I envision my hands rolling over his shoulders but I've never experienced emotional butterflies before.

After we did all of Kyle's laundry, for the record he was the one to stop our makeout session to get back to folding, we took his clothes upstairs to his apartment, and walked back to my place. My roommate is back home for the weekend so my place is not only pretty tidy but it doesn't smell like weed. Well not as strongly of weed at least.

Kyle waited for me while I showered. Part of me wanted him to join me but it's also kind of hot knowing he knows I'm in here.

Naked.

Wet.

Soapy?

I'm a nerd.

I laugh at myself because of my own train of thought while standing in front of my closet in my towel.

Kyle walks into my room and leans against the door frame. "Closet full of clothes and nothing to wear?" He says with a smile.

"Something like that. I'm trying to decide."

"That one." He says with a nod towards my entire closet.

"What 'one'? There are like 50 things hanging here!" I say with an exasperated laugh.

"The yellow one." The one I wore to the bar the night we saw his band play. The night he broke up with Tiffany.

"Yeah?"

"Yeah." He says with a heat to his tone I didn't know voices could make.

"Alright. Decision made."

He turns on his heel to leave the room but then pivots right back and crosses over to me. He grabs my waist and pulls me close to him. I gasp a breath.

"It's driving me crazy knowing you're naked under this towel." He whispers into my ear as his finger runs along the top of the towel, which is, incidentally, the top of my breasts.

I nuzzle into his neck, smile, and then gently push him away.

"Easy there cowboy." I giggle. "Go away and let me get dressed."

He slunks comedically out of the room before sneaking a peek back in.

I roll my eyes, smile, and get dressed.

Kyle's arms are full of grocery bags as he backs into his apartment, holding the door open for me with his body. I've got a bottle of wine and some flowers he slipped into the cart while we were getting ingredients for dinner. He is going to make a pasta dish and he seems totally fine with the fact that I have zero interest in cooking.

The kiss we shared this morning in his laundry room is all the kissing we've done today. Thankfully, not all the touching. He put his hand on my lower back as we moved through doors or around other people on the sidewalk. He ran his hand up my back and let it rest at the nape of my neck as we ordered coffees. I think my skin will forever remember the way his finger tip felt as it traveled across the top of my towel.

Each of these quick connections has me craving more. The kiss we shared this morning was so sweet and gentle and hot and electrifying and I can't imagine what a whole night being together would be like.

Oh wait, yes I can.

A bloom of tingly feelings rush through my body.

I have to clamp my thighs together, afraid they'll start shaking and give me away.

And I then blush.

I can feel the heat rising and it feels like the room has turned pink.

"Whaa-aat?" Kyle asks with curiosity.

Omigosh he saw me blush. "Oh, urm, nothing." This comes out at an alarmingly high pitch. I laugh nervously. "Nothing." I say again, in a deeper voice, as I clear my throat.

"Doesn't seem like 'nothing'."

"Well it's not *nothing*, nothing but it's nothing I want to talk about."

We're locked in this eye contact thing and I'm either going to run away with some crazy excuse or jump on him like I'm a blanket and he's on fire.

I don't think I'm breathing. At least not regularly.

Keeping my gaze he slides his hand that's on the counter closer and it meets mine.

FIRE! FIRE!

I step in and before I can take a breath he has closed the distance between us and his lips are on mine.

Gentle, yes, but strong with an urgency that wasn't there before. The hand that was on the counter is now at the small of my back. Fingers splayed wide, pulling me into him. His other hand is on my neck. His thumb comes under my jaw and he moves my head to the side and places kisses down my neck.

I'd like to say that my breath catches like the cute main characters in romance novels but no, I am gasping for air like a fish out of water.

My hands have moved to his chest and I can feel his heartbeat. I want to get closer. Feel his skin. So I lower my hands slowly to where his t-shirt ends and then slide them back up his abdomen under his shirt.

Now it's his turn to gasp.

I want to freeze this moment. But I can't wait to explore more. His skin is soft and warm. His muscles taught and firm. I want to rest my cheek against his chest. Nuzzle him. I want to know if his body feels like a being in a comfy chair under a blanket on a rainy day.

He slowly pulls me with him to the sofa. Before he sits down he tugs his t-shirt off over his head by tugging on the collar. How he manages to get his shirt off like that is a mystery but I am thankful for the chance to see his arms above his head like that.

I am greedily taking in the sight of him when he spins me around and begins to untie the back of my dress, slowly. He trails his finger across my back as he does it and I feel radiating tingles throughout my body. I shift my weight from side to side as his hands guide the dress off my hips to the ground. He turns me around then sits back to take me all in.

"Liz, you're so beautiful." It's almost a whisper.

I am standing between his legs in my bra and panties and I bend down to kiss him. His hands find my rib cage, he pulls, and I straddle his lap. Instinctively his hands find my ass. He groans.

"What was that for?" I ask as I move to kiss his neck.

"I have admired this ass on several occasions."

I sit back and laugh. I meet his gaze. "No way."

"Yes way. The first time you came to see the band play I admired your ass in that dress before I knew it was you."

I smile, remembering that night. Thinking about how we got from there to here in a few short weeks. How this feels so right. So natural. How any other scenario seems absurd.

"I can't believe we're doing this." He whispers.

"Me either. But we are, aren't we?"

"Yeah, we are." And his grip tightens as he kisses me again. My legs are wobbling already but his steady grip anchors me. I can tell Kyle knows what to do with his hands. And he's hardly done anything yet. I mean we're still in the over-the-bra second base territory here.

Nevermind.

His thumb slips into my bra cup and he folds it down revealing my nipple. He looks up at me and then puts his mouth on my breast while folding the cup down off my other breast. There's both a hunger and a reverence to his actions. He slides his hand around my back, unhooks my bra and then helps me slide it down my arms while pulling me into another kiss.

Bra cast aside he moves back to my breasts, pulling the other into his mouth. Each grip, each caress, sends a flood of need to my core. My hands are raking through his hair and I try to pull him back up to kiss me but he doesn't let me.

He pulls back and kisses the space between my breasts and moves one hand up to my neck and the other under my knee and in some sort of modified wrestling move he has me on my back. I can't help it, I giggle.

"Too much?" He asks, breathless.

"No, just right." I smile and he kisses me again.

This is the first time he's been on top of me. I feel surrounded by him and completely safe. With my hands splayed wide to feel as much of him as I can, I move my hands up his chest. I catch a nipple in the process and he hisses.

"Too much?" I ask with a smile.

"No, just right." He replies before leaning back over me and continuing to drive me wild by sucking and nipping around my breasts.

I wrap my legs around his waist, hooking them at the ankles behind him. He comes up to kiss me and moves his hands to my knees. He sits back again so I unhook my legs and he presses my legs open and looks down at me. He slides his hands down the backs of my thighs to the waistband of my underwear. I tilt my hips up just enough for him to pull my underwear off.

He rolls the fabric down my legs and carefully pulls my feet through. His strong hands hold one leg at the ankle and pushes the other open to the side. I am spread wide for him. Bare.

Self consciousness creeps in. I can stay in the moment when it's hot and heavy and we're kissing so I don't have to think about what he's thinking about but laid out like this with him looking at me all my insecurities come rushing to the front of my mind.

"Don't." He says as he brings his gaze up to mine.

"Don't what?"

"Don't think so much."

"Then kiss me."

He leans down and places a kiss on my neck right behind my ear. It almost tickles but it definitely sends a ripple of electricity through me. I arch my back and my breasts press into his chest. He kisses me again but he starts to move across my jaw back to my mouth.

This next kiss is urgent. He's pushing my mouth open wider and as our tongues collide I rake my hands down his back. He pulls up and presses himself into me. The pressure of his jeans on my bare slit creates friction like striking a match and I tilt my hips looking for more.

"Easy Liz." He says as he starts to pull back. I reach for the button of his jeans but he moves my hands away and down to my sides. Pinning me there. My legs curl around his and he bends to place a kiss on my stomach.

Slowly he releases my wrists from where they were pinned at my sides and drags his hand down my belly, past my pelvic bone, to my center. He slips one arm under my thigh and pulls me open. The thumb on his other hand massages over my slit.

"Yes, Kyle." I whimper. My eyes flutter closed. My focus on where his one hand is holding me down and his other is rubbing me up. I gasp in surprise as he places a kiss on my inner thigh. Then another.

"Oh my god, Kyle." I moan when his tongue swipes up my slit in a broad stroke, ending with a tap on my clit. Arousal floods through me, pooling at my center but creating a pulsing sensation that is building with each pass of his tongue.

My arms start to flail and I cross them over my face as a sensation I've never experienced before rushes through my body. My legs are shaking. My breath is short. The concentration of pleasure in the pit of my stomach is almost painful but the lightness I feel everywhere else balances out the intensity.

Kyle increases his pace and my hands land in his hair. He continues to hold me open as my legs ache to clench together around him.

The pressure in my pelvis builds to a point and I'm pressing his head into me as the sensation of his connection with me rolls through my body.

My blood is on fire and then suddenly my world explodes and a lightness overtakes me.

"Oh my, ah fuck, Kyle!" I scream as I arch my back, gripping his hair to keep him where he is as he pulls me through my orgasm with his tongue. He slowly, gently, strokes me with his thumb as he places kisses to my pelvis, my stomach before coming to rest his chin on my chest.

I look down at him as I try to catch my breath. His eyes are wild but there is a satisfaction as well. I've never had a guy bring me to completion like that before. It's always been a few perfunctory licks and then on to the main event. I bring my hands to his face, his jaw, and pass my thumb over his lips. He nibbles at my finger and then slides up further to kiss me.

When he pulls up and rests his forehead to mine his bulge presses into my leg. I reach down and through his jeans I cup him and he presses further into my hand. I sit up a little further and reach for his button again. This time he lets me and I slowly unbutton his jeans and pull his cock out of the waistband of his boxer briefs.

I give him a little push on the chest and he sits back on his haunches before I push again and he rolls back to lay on the sofa. I grab his jeans and tug them down. He lifts his ass in the air so I can pull his boxer briefs off too. I'm positioned between his legs, sitting on my knees. I reach out and grip his erection near the base and pull my hand up to where I pass my thumb gently over the head of his penis. As I drag my hand back down he presses up into my hand seeking out more friction.

His eyes are closed and he lets out a soft grunt as I press my thumb between his balls. His hips buck up and then his hands grab my arms.

"Up here now." He says and he pulls me up to his torso. He begins to kiss me as I straddle him and I feel his erection jump and twitch against my ass. He curls up, reaches for his jeans and pulls a condom out of his pocket. He kisses me and I lift up enough for him to roll the condom over his length.

Kyle moves his hands to my hips and with my hand at the base of his cock he lowers me down, inch by magnificent inch. My hands move to his chest to brace myself. The feeling of him inside me brings the next round of arousal to my core. His grip on my hips is strong as he rolls me forwards and back. He is fully contained in me and my orgasm is building again.

He bends his knees and lifts his hips to drive into me even further. I let out a moan of pleasure as he hits a place inside me I didn't know was there. Then he starts to pull me off him and I whimper in protest before he pulls my hips back down while pushing his up.

"Oh fuck!" I yell out as my pussy clenches around him.

"Fuck, yes, so good Liz. I feel you. You feel so good." He says as he pulls me up and brings me down again.

I sit up straight and his hands move to my breasts where he cups me and then rolls my nipples through his fingers. I clench around him again as I feel the pressure building again in my pelvis.

"Oh god, I'm close again Kyle." I say as I lean forward and pump myself on him.

He grunts as he grabs my hips and increases his pace. I fall forward again, unable to hold myself up, and he wraps his arms around my waist and pumps up into me over and over.

"Liz, oh shit." He says as he squeezes his eyes closed tighter. I pull up and put my hands on his shoulders which again changes the angle as he continues to drive in and out.

His grip on me is powerful. His action is consuming. My walls are tightening around him and when he slides his hand between us and places his thumb on my clit I fall over the edge.

"Ah, fuck, Kyle!" I yell out as he massages my bundle of nerves and continues to thrust into me before he stills and grips me tighter.

"Oh fuck, Liz." He whispers as he exhales. His hands journeying up from my legs to my ribs as I collapse on top of him.

Our bodies slow and eventually our breathing slows down too. He slides to the side so I can fall to the sofa next to him before he stands and walks to the bathroom. He washes up and comes back to me where he takes my hand and pulls me up.

"Do your legs work?" He teases.

"Barely. Yours."

"No, I can't feel them at all. C'mon" And he pulls me by the hand to the bathroom.

I step inside, he pulls the door and says "I'll meet you in bed" as it closes.

After I pee, I stand at the sink and look at the girl in the mirror. She is full of color, her eyes are sparkling, and she now knows what two orgasms in a row feels like.

Feels incredible if you're wondering.

When I step out of the bathroom Kyle is sitting in his bed and he has pulled back the covers on my side. I climb in to join him and we lay down. His arm slides under the pillow and around my shoulders as I curl into him and place my hand on his chest.

He lets out a sigh and turns his head in my direction. I look up at him and a million questions run through my mind. Was it good for him? Will we do it again? Did I do it right? Was I too rough?

"Liz," he starts and I look up at him. He's smiling, almost laughing. "Don't start."

"How do you know?"

"You get this little crease right here," he puts his finger between my eyebrows, "when you start asking a million questions in your head. I find it endearing but I don't want you questioning anything right now. If that was half as good for you as it was for me we're going to be just fine." He says as he slides his hand down my side and squeezes my ass.

I tuck my face into his chest and smile. I had no idea sex could be like that. That it could be such a powerful experience. And on our first time too. It was like he knew exactly what to do with my body, things I didn't even know I needed, and surrendering to him wasn't even a conscious thought. He commanded it with his hold on me and how much I trust him.

Just thinking about it is sending waves of arousal through me. I rub my thighs together trying to relieve some of the tension building again.

Kyle notices. He raises an eyebrow at me.

I cover my face to hide my grin and he pulls my hands away and presses his lips to mine.

"Whatcha thinking there pretty girl?"

Deciding it's time to offer up some of my vulnerability I tell the truth.

"I didn't know it could feel that good." I say while looking down his torso and tracing my fingers across his stomach.

He reaches down and tilts my chin up to him so we're looking at each other.

"Just wait, it'll get better."

CHAPTER 29

KYLE

Waking up next to Liz is the most incredible feeling in the world. I feel protective and protected all at once. She fell asleep with her head on my chest, her arm around my torso, and my arms wrapped around her. Over the course of the night she rolled away but never far. I stir and flip my pillow over to feel the cool side and fold it to hold up my head and neck while I lay on my side.

"Hey," she rasps without opening her eyes.

"Hey," I whisper as I lean down to kiss her temple.

"That was, umm, I dunno, pretty great."

"Ha yeah. I agree 'pretty great'."

Understatement of the year. This was the best sex of my life. Not that I've had a lot of experience but it is tough for me to imagine it could get better. Liz responded to me in ways no girl has before and I could tell she truly surrendered to the things the two of us were doing together.

"I'm going to get a glass of water, can I get you one too?"

"Mhmm," she sighs and I can't help but grin like the cat who got the mouse.

When I return with the water she is sitting up with the sheet covering her breasts. Those breasts. I can still feel their weight in my palm from when she was on top of me last night and as soon as I think about it I feel myself plump a degree.

I slide into bed next to her and she moves over under my arm after taking a sip of water. Her fingers are tracing circles on my stomach. "Stop that. It tickles."

"Oh does it?" She says, raising one eyebrow and pushing up on her elbow to look me in the eyes.

"Yes it does. Don't start something you can't finish."

"Who, me?" She bats her eyelashes as she sits up. And then she grins and brings both her hands to my stomach and starts tickling.

"I warned you!" I growl before I grab her wrists and move over her. Balancing myself on my knees and elbows while holding her wrists pinned down beside her head.

Her eyes are sparkling and I can see her trying to figure out her next move. She is so playful and flirty and I love it. I love her.

I love her.

My face must give me away because Liz's expression changes towards concern.

"What's wrong?" She asks.

"Absolutely nothing." I whisper. I see the sparkle return to her eyes and together our smiles turn into grins. I lean down and kiss her and we laugh into each other's kisses. It's like we've both realized at the same time how giddy we are. I keep her wrists pinned under my hands and bend down to nip her breasts. They're pulled up at the moment and the tender skin under them is exposed and calling for my attention.

"Hey no fair!" she giggles.

"All's fair in love and war," I say as I lick around her navel.

Her underwear is already off because she never put it back on again last night. She's acting like we could start things up again but I don't want to push my luck.

"May I?" I ask as I slide one hand down her arm, across her chest and stomach, and don't stop.

"Mhmm," she manages with a nod of her head.

I like her stretched out like this so I leave my other hand where it is pinning her and I slide the two fingers of my free hand down the outside of her entrance and back up gently over her slit.

Her breath is ragged and I know I'm onto something. I repeat the move again and she starts to roll her hips into my hand. I'm kissing the side of her neck and breathing in her smell. She wants more, and quickly, but I know better.

Last night I tried to go slow. I tried to savor it. But once I was inside her I couldn't hold back. I drove into her again and again and silently prayed that the pace was working for her. When I entered her again later in bed I was able to go slower, to feel myself contained in her. I wonder what she likes in the morning.

I've let her wrists go and her hands find their way to my shoulders. She pulls herself up to kiss me and I slide an arm around her back to hold her up. I want to stay right here. With her in my arms, with her taste on my lips. Her eyes close as we breathe in sync, already having found our rhythm together.

I think since the first time I saw her I knew she was a special person. Someone that would fit into my world and become a fixture. That's exactly what is happening. To my core I understand that Liz and I are meant to be together. We were meant to meet. Meant to become friends. Meant to become more.

I am trailing kisses down her jaw towards her ear, a soft moan escapes her lips. It sends shivers down my spine. Already addicted to her I slowly kiss down her neck to her collar bone to her shoulder. I glance up at Liz and her eyes are closed. She seems entirely lost in the moment.

Sitting back on my haunches I allow her to fall back down to the bed. She opens her eyes and lifts an eyebrow to question what I'm doing. I crawl up next to her and prop myself up on one elbow while I move my other hand down between her legs again. She exhales and tilts her chin up, arching her back which puts her breasts on full display.

I begin to massage her clit with light pressure and within a few seconds her hips are bucking looking for more. She rolls towards me and grabs my neck to pull me in for a kiss. I give her one quickly and then urge her back down on the bed.

"Why won't you kiss me?" She asks, while her hips continue to roll under my touch.

"Because I want to watch you come on my fingers." I tell her by dipping close to her ear. Her eyes fly open and she looks at me. I'm sure guys she's been with before haven't paid full attention to her. I've learned enough in my time to know that women will come multiple times while in bed with me. And while penetration feels incredible for my body, hers needs to be caressed, treasured, and pleasured.

She's still looking at me so I place a soft kiss on her eyebrow, forcing her eyes to close.

"But what about you?" And she reaches down to put my cock in her hands.

I roll my hips out of the way and mutter. "Just relax and feel everything Liz." While I place another kiss on her forehead.

She takes a deep breath and I continue to massage her pussy. I circle her clit, changing the pressure each time. Softer first, then harder, and then softer again. I slide my fingers down her slit to her backside and back up feeling her get wetter each time.

I focus back on the little nub at her center and her legs begin shaking.

"Oh fuck. Oh my god." She mutters as she bites her bottom lip. Her hands are gripping the sheets, she's white knuckling it. She's close.

"Ah, shit… I'm close."

I increase the speed and pressure of my fingers on her clit.

"Kyle! Oh… oh!" She yelps out. "It's too much!"

I want to say something to soothe her but I know as soon as I do her mind will be pulled from the bliss she's experiencing. Instead I steady my own breathing and continue to bring her to the end of her rope. A flush has appeared on her chest which is rolling up and down with her hips and she searches for the right amount of friction.

"Oh… oh… Kyle! Oh my god!" She exclaims and clenches her thighs together. The look on her face is one of pure pleasure.

Bliss.

Relief.

And I did that for her. I was able to deliver that whole body euphoria.

She returns to earth and rolls towards me, I skim my hand up her hip to her waist. She reaches up and kisses me, her tongue asking for entry. I slide my arm under her shoulders and pull her in close to me while we deepen our kiss.

"I want to have some witty banter but I can't come up with anything. I think you broke my brain." She says as she lays her head on my shoulder.

"I can't even say I'm sorry for doing that. You're so fucking beautiful my brain is broken too."

I feel her smile into my chest and I press a kiss to the top of her head.

We lay there for a little longer, our breathing in sync, and I don't know if

I've ever been this relaxed in my life. I'm drifting off to sleep when Liz slides out of bed.

"Where do you think you're going?" I ask her as I prop myself up on one elbow.

"I am going to the shower." She says with the raise of one eyebrow before twirling away and closing the door behind her.

Another day together. On paper it would read as ordinary; shower sex, bagels, laundry, getting ready for the week.

But this day is extraordinary.

(You saw shower sex in the list right?)

I've spent the day with Liz. We've laughed, we've been comfortably quiet together. I feel energized in her presence. The dinner we didn't get to last night is on the stove now. Liz is taking pillows out to the fire escape for us to eat al-fresco.

"You sure you don't mind if these are outside?"

"Nah, they were hand-me-downs from my Grandma."

"Really?" Liz takes a second look at the pillows. "Your grandma has surprisingly masculine taste."

I chuckle. "I can't be sure but I'd bet my Grandma bought them new for me but didn't want me to think she was being extravagant so she called them hand-me-down."

"That's sweet." Liz comes back to the kitchen and takes a plate and wine glass with her out the window. She sets them down and then picks up her camera.

We stopped at her apartment after breakfast this morning so she could change clothes, start laundry, and get her camera. While her clothes were in the dryer she used my running shoes to take some photos she said would work for a personal trainer, coach, or fitness podcaster. I became absorbed in her process. Just like at the beach she would set up a little scene, take a picture, adjust the scene, take another picture. It took all of ten minutes but she had several different shots she would edit and upload.

At first I thought the pictures looked the same but then she explained how one was portrait, one landscape, one square, one with negative space at the top, one at the bottom, and one where the items were arranged around the outside so someone could add text in the middle.

I'm standing at the window watching her work, a faint smile on her face. I'm holding my plate and wine glass waiting for her to take a photo of the set up. She looks up at me. The smile disappears instantly.

"Oh shit, I'm sorry. I didn't realize you were waiting. Here." She rushes to move the plate to the side.

"Are you done?"

"Yeah, I can be." And I can hear some disappointment in her voice.

"Liz," but she doesn't look up at me. She is staring down at her lap so I reach up and lift her chin so she's facing me. Her eyes are still downcast.

"Liz." My tone is stern enough for her to look me in the eye.

"Are you finished taking photos of this fun fire-escape date you set up?"

"Yeah."

"Don't lie to me." I widen my eyes so she knows I'm serious even though I kept my tone playful.

"I'm not lying, I can be done. It isn't important that I take four more variations of the same photo."

"But do you want to?"

"Kyle, c'mon it's fine. Let's eat."

I don't know what to do here. She clearly wants to keep taking photos but she is telling me she doesn't. She picks up her plate but doesn't start eating. She's just poking the food with her fork.

"Why won't you tell me you want to take more pictures?" I ask right before putting a forkful of pasta in my mouth.

"Because it's not important."

"What do you mean?" I say this as I chew. My mother definitely taught me better but I've gotta keep her talking.

"I dunno, you cooked this whole meal for me and instead of just enjoying it I'm taking pictures of it." Liz says to her lap.

"But that's what you do." I say as I set my fork down.

"No, what I do is intern at Fosters, hopefully getting a job offer from them this week which will launch my successful career in professional fundraising." She's still talking to her lap. "The photography is just a hobby."

"Why do you do that?"

"Do what?" She looks up at me.

"That." I say while kind of motioning to her. "You duck your head and then disregard your passion, your talent. You talk down about this unique skill you have to capture images people want to use. That people pay for. Stop it. Stop not believing in yourself. Even if you get the Fosters job, which I'm sure you will, you can continue doing the photography. Fosters is going to be so boring day-in and day-out, photography can be your outlet."

Liz's body is still as she sits there looking at me. I can't believe I said all of that. And I think my face says as much. Her face is unreadable and now I'm worried that I went too far.

"Nevermind, I took that too far. I just don't like to see you frowning."

"No, it's okay. I didn't realize how much I was doing it." She finally takes a bite of her pasta. She looks out over the railing while she chews. I know her mind is working because that little crease is between her eyebrows and I want to know what's going on in there. I'm about to ask when she swallows and turns towards me.

"Thank you for calling me out on that. I've been doing it for years. Downplaying my interest in art because it's not a 'real job' or accommodating others' needs before my own." She pauses. " Truth?" She looks at me and I nod. "I did want to take a few more photos. But I'm enjoying having dinner with you out here more." She smiles softly and I feel myself smiling back.

"We can plan a re-do next weekend."

"It's a date." Liz replies with a mouthful of pasta.

I catch the surprise in her eyes as the word "date" slipped out of her mouth. Like she's questioning if she just scared me away. Little does she know I'm already there. I like the idea of dating her. I like the idea of a lot more with her but dating is as good a place as any to start. I want to put her at ease, I hate seeing her worked up, stressed, anxious. I smile and pop out a quick "yep" before taking another bite of pasta.

"So, is it gonna be weird tomorrow?" she asks after we've finished dinner. I want to say it won't be but I'm going to find myself looking for opportunities to make eye contact, to brush our fingers together as I hand her something, and enjoy the flush of her cheeks if someone asks how her weekend was.

"Eh, maybe a little. Mostly because I'm going to want to pick you up and run you back to my apartment instead of watching you have to do mindless shit all day."

"Stop. I mean it. It isn't against the rules for interns to date but it still feels very close to a code of conduct issue." She is concentrating on picking her cuticle. I can tell it's to help settle the nervous energy in her stomach. I have it too. But there's less on the line for me because I don't need an offer from Fosters. The least I can do is try to be calm and steady for her.

"Liz, it'll be fine. It's only a few more days anyways." I reach over and pick up her plate then crawl back through the window. She picks up the wine glasses and follows.

"You wash, I'll dry?" I ask as I sling a dish cloth over my shoulder. I turn around and find her leaning against the counter, setting the wine glasses down carefully. She's not making eye contact but she is smiling. Then I see her skin flush from her cheeks to her neck and I have a feeling I know what she's thinking about.

"On second thought, dishes can wait." I cross over to the counter and step behind her. I slide my hands down her sides and catch her hips. She presses back into me and I lean forward to kiss the side of her neck.

"You sure? There are a lot of dishes here." She says as she tries to take a step towards the sink. I tighten my grip to let her know just how sure I am.

"Yeah. I'm sure."

I like the feeling of her backside pressing against my cock so I lean in a little, trapping her between the counter and my body. My hands are holding her hips and I continue to kiss up and down her neck. Her hands float up above her head and around to my hair where she holds us in place.

Wanting her mouth, I turn her towards me and press into her again. She loops her arms around my neck and I hitch her up to the countertop. I hold her on the edge so our bodies continue to connect. She slips her fingers down inside my collar and I step back to pull my t-shirt off and toss it to the side.

Her hands roam my shoulders, down my chest to my stomach where she slides them around to my back and pulls me in for a kiss. She scrapes her nails down my back and I let out a hiss at the combination of pleasure and pain that she produced.

"You okay?" She asks.

"More than okay." I reassure her. Hell, I want her to do that again and again. I want to be marked by her, claimed. I want to do the same.

I break our kiss and move to her neck and nip and suck my way to her shoulder, thankful for the off-the-shoulder top she wore today. Liz's nails scrape down my back again and I nip her a little harder and she hisses before exhaling.

Returning my way back up to her neck, she shifts on the counter and opens her legs wider. Welcoming me. I kiss her under her jaw, and down the other side of her neck to her shoulder and run my hands up the top of her thighs. Her jean shorts are so short I can reach the point on her hip where her underwear should be and there's nothing.

"Liz, are you wearing any underwear?"

She looks at me and catches her smile in her lip. I fixate on her teeth sinking into her own flesh, swollen from my kisses, when she slowly shakes her head no as an answer to my question. I can't stop myself and I grip her hips tighter. Quickly I unbutton her shorts and slide them down her legs. Immediately I move one hand to her center. I drag my thumb up along her slit to find her already soaking.

"You're already wet for me?" I whisper into her ear before letting my teeth graze along her ear lobe.

Liz can't seem to speak so she nods and then reaches forwards to unbutton my shorts. She pushes them off my ass and I step out of them and kick them to the side. Her top is gathered together and stretchy where it hugs her every curve. I simply pull the top of the dress down to reach her tits.

She isn't wearing a bra either so pulling down her top frees her and she arches her back pushing her breasts into my hands. I know she's wet and ready but I want to make this last for us so I focus on massaging her tits and sucking on her nipples, bringing the little nubs out to play.

"Oh Kyle. Yes." She moans as she brings her arms up over my shoulders.

Suddenly she hooks her legs together behind me and pulls me into her. My cock twitches when he feels her wet pussy through my boxer briefs. She rolls her hips to create friction and my balls swell as tension builds in my low back.

"Liz, hold on." I plead knowing I won't last if she continues to move herself along me.

"Ugh, I need you in me now." She says as her heels dig into my ass.

Can't hear that enough. I break our embrace and make sure she isn't going to fall off the counter when I step back. "Stay there." I tell her.

She nods and brings her own hands to her breasts where she rolls her nipples between her fingers and, fuck me, I almost shoot off right there.

My condoms are in my dresser drawer so I reach in to get one and turn around to find her head thrown back while she continues to play with her own tits. I almost trip over myself as I step back to her, slide my boxers off, and roll the condom on.

When I grab her hips to tilt her in my direction she moves her hands to the counter behind her.

"No, keep playing with your tits."

Liz looks at me and does what I tell her to do while I grip the base of my erection and drive into her. I keep a hold of her hips and thrust in and out at a feverish pace.

"Oh fuck, Kyle!"

"I know babe, I know." I grunt out moving one arm around her back to help hold her exactly where I need her.

Liz's hands still as she bites her lip and lets out little whimpers with each push from me.

"Your pussy is so tight, warm. So fucking good." I tell her as I look down and watch myself move in and out of her.

"Kyle… oh… I– I'm close."

"I know babe." I can feel her clenching around me. "Me too."

She moves her arms up over my shoulders and hugs my neck bringing our bodies together. I grip her ass as every cell in my body explodes with my ejaculation.

I can't feel my legs so I release her from my grip and palm the counter still inside her. She curls back and kisses my neck and runs her hands down my arms. Once I catch my breath I pull out, help her down, and go to clean up in the bathroom.

When I come out she's standing with her top pulled back up over her tits and her shorts are back on. She's holding my boxer briefs out to me and they're swinging on her finger. I take them from her and slide them back on, my cock still half hard. She walks around the counter to the sink while I put my shorts back on.

"Agatha was right."

"What?"

"Agatha Sanderson. She told me that playing with my nipples in front of you would drive you wild. She was right."

I never thought I'd be thankful to an octogenarian for sex tips but, yeah, thank you Agatha Sanderson.

"Now, keep that shirt off and you'll wash, *I'll* dry."

CHAPTER 30

LIZ

This past week with Kyle has helped to keep my nerves under control. He's been able to distract me from the looming deadline at the end of the week. But, there's nothing that can calm me down now. Today is the day. Decision Day. I find out if I have a job and future in the city. If my career is off to a solid start. If my dreams are about to come true. We've spent a grueling 8 weeks note-taking, proofreading, researching and stapling and I'm sure we've learned something about professional fundraising along the way but I couldn't tell you what it was.

Hopefully there isn't a quiz.

I spent more time than normal on my hair and makeup today. Maybe I should have spent this same amount of time all summer long? Maybe they'll notice that my hair is smooth today when it's been pulled back into a ratty overly dry shampooed bun most other days.

I haven't been perfect this summer. Judy had to make corrections on a few of the reports I proofread first which I think is a tally in my con column. Thankfully Kyle hasn't said anything about my mistake with the cover sheets for the reports. He could have easily mentioned it in his weekly one-on-one and Judy would have had my neck.

It's too late to worry now. I don't have enough information to worry anyways.

All week it has been a struggle not to turn to goo with Kyle in the room. He has snuck more than a few winks at me and I felt my core tighten a little each time. Chandler is oblivious. Nora seems a little suspicious but hasn't said anything.

After today we won't have to worry about what people at work think. We won't see each other all day long but I think that'll work in our favor. I'll be craving him by 6pm. And also craving the dinner he makes. I think in the last week I've had more proper meals than all summer combined.

Last night after we left work we stopped at my place for a change of clothes and then went to his place. He made me a plate of salmon, vegetables, and rice in some sort of sauce that involved mustard and mayo and maple syrup. Don't ask me how it worked but it did. Incredible. We ate and then did the dishes together. It wasn't tossing bubbles at each other or spraying each other with the nozzle but there were plenty of giggles and hip bumps.

After dinner he turned on a baseball game and I pulled up my laptop to edit the images from the fire escape dinner. He reset the scene for me on Monday night so I could take the photos again. He also then sent me the names of two different photographers who have built stock image catalogs and are now hired by companies for photoshoots.

It's been a week of dating but I think back to how he's been supportive all summer. How he has encouraged me. And doubted my doubt. He makes me feel like I can believe in myself.

This is the thought I carry with me as I stroll into the lobby. I tap my badge and confidently walk through the security gate. I turn to smile at Joe the security guard and then it happens.

I wipe out.

Ass over ankles.

Completely on my face. I honestly can't explain what happened. Walking one minute, eating shit the next. My shoe is clinging onto one toe. My bag has slid into the elevator that opened at the same moment and stops when it hits some really nice shoes.

I look up from the shoes to the pants to the suit coat to the face and it's Marcus, of all people. He sees me on the ground and with a worried look steps out quickly of the elevator and reaches for my arm to help me stand up.

At the same moment I hear Kyle behind me saying "Liz! Are you OK?"

and then his hand is on my arm helping me up. As I stand back up I'm trying to smile but I can feel the hot tears building up already. Marcus lets go to pick up my bag and hand it to me and as I take a step I wince in pain.

Kyle's grip on my arm gets tighter and he leans down to say, "I think it's your knee."

"Oh, nah, I'm sure it's fine. Thanks." I say to Marcus who has handed me my bag and ID badge.

"I can't believe that happened again." Kyle says, to himself but loud enough that both Marcus and I heard it.

My head turns towards him in shock. *Again?* He knows that I fell before? How? I have only told Nora. She wouldn't have told people, would she? There's no way. She's competitive but not so much that she'd share embarrassing stories about me at the office. My mind is reeling with how Kyle knows and the shame all but makes me nauseous.

"Again? You've fallen like this before?" Marcus says as he straightens his suit sleeves and brushes his hands off.

Shit.

Marcus now has seen me wipe out and heard I've done it before.

Don't cry.

It would be disastrous.

Don't barf.

That would be horrendous.

In through the nose…

Out through the mouth…

Repeat.

"Umm, ha, yeah, the same thing happened when I came in for my interview."

Say something witty…

"Must be the shoes!"

"I've got to run to a meeting, but Kyle, can you help her get upstairs?" Marcus says as Kyle helps me limp to the elevator.

KYLE

I am irrationally annoyed that Marcus asked me to help Liz. Of course I'm going to help her, and I'm going to better understand the nature of her injury before treating it, dick. I don't need some guy who thinks he's a golden child to tell me to do any of that.

Also I might be misdirecting my concern for Liz into annoyance with Marcus.

I had to stifle an eye roll and mentally unclench my fist that felt ready to cock. I might not want to work here but I don't want to make any enemies either.

Liz is clearly limping and I'm doing my best to check out her leg without, you know *checking out her leg*. I can see that her knee is already swollen.

"Here, sit down, elevate your leg and I'll get you some ice."

"OK Bossy. It's not a big deal, I'm fine."

"No, you're not. That knee is twisted, maybe sprained and you need RICE."

"Not hungry, thanks."

"No *RICE*." I say with emphasis.

"Yeaaah, it's like 8am. I'm not interested in eating rice."

"Rest, Ice, Compression and Elevation. R. I. C. E., RICE. It's a first aid protocol for twists and sprains."

"Oh," Liz says with a giggle. "How do you know that?"

"I'm an Eagle Scout."

She looks at me with an understanding expression and says, "That explains so much."

"What do you mean?"

"Oh, sorry. I didn't mean for that to sound, I dunno, bratty. I grew up with a lot of Eagle Scouts and camp counselors and it just makes a lot of sense. You're hard working, prepared, quiet but confident and when I add in that you're trained in first aid," she looks at her open hand like it's a calculator, "Yep. Adds up to Eagle Scout."

I look at Liz and can see that she's let her guard down. She's trying to sound flippant but the things she has noticed about me are what I pride myself on. And protecting. I would do anything to protect Liz, physically and emotionally. My stomach plummeted when I saw her slip in the lobby today. I couldn't reach her fast enough to catch her fall.

I can see a bruise starting but I don't want to tell her because she's looking straight at me and I can see some of her embarrassment is gone. "This doesn't look too bad. One summer when I was a pack leader at camp

I saw a lot worse. Kids getting their legs caught in kayaks or busted up falling out of trees."

"You were a counselor at scout camp?"

"Yeah, for the last two summers of undergrad."

"Well who would have thunk it! I was a counselor at the camp in our town. Those summers were the best. Way better than being a Fosters intern."

"At least we're done interning today." And a wave of disappointment washes over me because I'm realizing again that things change for us after this. I love seeing Liz at work everyday. Maybe we don't need to see each other all day every day to have a strong relationship. But I don't want to be around anyone else. The idea is starting to make me feel emotional and I want to be strong for her.

"I'm going to go ask Deb for an ice pack." And I walk off taking a deep breath to steady my nerves because it feels like everything is about to change.

CHAPTER 31

LIZ

The physical pain I'm in is lessening the embarrassment I felt. Like it was all worth it because I really did get hurt. I can see the bruise forming and it is swollen but I have a feeling it would be worse if Kyle hadn't swooped in and RICEd the situation.

I've kept it elevated all day and he picked up a wrap bandage on his lunch break for me to use when I get home.

The Offer or No Offer, meetings are on our calendars. Chandler is first at 2:30, then Nora at 3. Me at 3:30 and Kyle at 4. It's going to be a long time to wait.

Chandler comes back into the conference room after his meeting and claps his hands together. He pauses in the doorway with his hands still together in front of him and says, "Well gang you're all still in the race. I didn't get a position."

He doesn't sound too beat up about it.

"I've been applying to other jobs the last few weeks. I'll stay with my parents until something works out." He finishes and then walks over to where his bag is already packed and slings the strap on his shoulder.

"I'm glad you're feeling good about it Chandler," Nora says as she stands up. She takes a deep breath "OK, me next! Here goes nothing."

We all kind of know she's going to get it. But we won't know for sure until she comes back in. Somehow 20 minutes pass with Chandler still wearing his bag on his shoulder while he tells us all about his weekend plans. Nora walks back in with a huge smile on her face.

"I got it! You're looking at the new Higher Education Associate for Fosters, Henderson & Associates!" She raises her hands in the air in triumph.

"Yay!! I'm so excited for you Nora!" I say and she gracefully walks over to me for a hug knowing I'm laid up.

She's wondering out loud where her office is going to be as I stand up to make my way to my meeting. I do my best to walk without a limp but I am not doing a good job of it. Slowly and somewhat sideways I make it to the board room. Inside James Foster himself is sitting at the table. His admin, Lauri, is off to his left in a chair along the wall. Marcus is to his right and Lauren is to his left.

I wave.

What the fuck am I doing?

Doofus.

Get it together.

I stuff the offending hand into my other hand and settle them in front of me as I take a seat on the near side of the table and Judy takes her seat next to Lauren.

Judy begins by introducing me to James and then she asks Marcus and Lauren to share their feedback about my performance.

I can't exactly process what they're saying. I'm still so nervous. I'll have to ask Lauri for her notes. After each of them take their turn James begins.

"Liz, I was impressed to hear what Marcus and Lauren had to say about your work and your enthusiasm. I know the internship is a lot of busywork," I flash a glance at Judy who frowns "but the Mercy presentation was high quality and everything else since has been acceptable.

"As an associate you'll be responsible for meeting with the clients and conveying our message. Sometimes clients don't want to hear it. Especially in medicine. All those doctors think they know better. We don't feel that you have the business decorum and communication skills we would expect of an associate."

He takes a breath and it sounds like a sigh when he exhales.

"Based on this we feel that you're not a fit for this firm going forward. We wish you luck in your future endeavors."

Wait, what?!

All the oxygen in the room suddenly disappears and my heart rate skyrockets.

What did he just tell me?

Before I have a chance to ask any follow up questions Judy stands and walks around the table to usher me out of the room.

I walk as quickly as I can back to the conference room. There's no sign of Kyle who I realize he is the only person I wanted to talk to at this moment. Nora is packed up and waiting for me. I try to smile.

"So?" She asks.

I open my mouth to speak but nothing comes out. Instead I slowly shake my head and slump down into my chair.

"Oh shit. Holy shit." Nora mutters as she drops her bag down onto the floor and kneels in front of my chair. "Are you okay? Are you gonna pass out? Scream? Break something? Because I would totally help you destroy the copy room right now."

I manage to chuckle because the idea of taking a baseball bat to the copy machine is tempting. Instead Nora grabs my bag, puts my things in it and says "Hold on." Before she walks out the door.

I wait in the conference room, totally stunned. And where is Kyle?

Nora walks back in looking over her shoulder.

"How fast can you move on that knee?"

"I dunno. Why?"

"Don't worry about it, just, umm, run." And Nora grabs my hand, both our bags, and pulls me down the hallway to the elevators. That's when I notice that my bag is full to the brim with snacks from the break room.

"Ohmigod I love you!" I giggle as the elevator doors open. We step inside and she hits the lobby button. Before I know it we're out on the sidewalk. My life is falling apart at the seams but I have a week's worth of snacks. I guess that's gotta count for something.

CHAPTER 32

LIZ

Nora brought me back to her apartment when we left Fosters. I've been in a daze, numb for the last few hours. Kyle has texted, and called, but I haven't answered. I don't know what to say to him.

I failed.

I let everyone down.

I let myself down.

I did call my parents to tell them. They were sympathetic and then immediately went into problem solving mode where they made the plans to come and pack me up for home this Thursday.

Six days until I move back home.

Nora slumps next to me on the sofa and hands me the open bottle of rosé. We didn't even bother with glasses.

Burritos have been ordered.

New Girl reruns are on TV.

"I feel bad that we're not out celebrating your job offer."

"Eh, who cares. Misery loves company."

My phone lights up on the table with another call from Kyle. Nora sees it, looks at me, and like a ninja she launches forward and answers it.

"Ky Ky whadduuupppp?" She hollers into the phone like a bad spring break DJ. She puts the phone on speaker as I sink further into the sofa, clutching the bottle to my chest.

"Nora? Hello? Is Liz there?"

"Yes, but unfortunately Liz is unable to come to the phone right now." Nora says in an overly polite voice. She twists to look at me and then says, "She's deep throating a bottle of rosé."

I was in fact taking a pull from the bottle but when she says this while staring at me I do a spit take, cough, and hold my hand out for the phone, wiping my mouth with the back of the hand holding the rosé.

"Ah, she couldn't take it anymore but here, she'll talk to you instead."

I take the phone and stand up to limp to Nora's bedroom.

"Liz? Hello? Where are you? Are you okay?"

"Hi Kyle, yeah, I'm fine. I'm at Nora's."

"What happened? I went to the bathroom and by the time I was back you were gone. Judy said you didn't get an offer? What the hell? Why not?"

"Yeah, I don't really want to talk about it. Congrats to you are in order though." My sarcasm is thick.

"Don't be like that. You know I didn't take the job."

"Yeah but you got the offer. That's all I wanted. I wanted the chance to prove myself. To be good enough to get the one thing I wanted." I have to stop because the tears are clogging my throat. Things are working out for everyone around me and I am the one who has to head home with my tail between my legs.

"Liz–"

"I gotta go. I'll call you later." I end the call before he can say anything else. It hurts too much.

I'm embarrassed.

Ashamed.

I can't tell him that I didn't get the job because of my *business decorum and communication skills*. I walk back out to the main room where Nora has dumped out all the snacks from our bags.

"So, is Kyle coming over?"

"No."

"Oh," She pauses. She's still sorting the snacks when she continues, "I thought you were, like, together."

"He told you?"

"No. I saw you two kissing on the sidewalk after work. It was a few blocks away from the building but yeah, caught ya." She clicks her tongue and gives me a double finger gun salute.

"Well shit. Then, yeah, I guess, we're together. Or we were together. Now, I dunno. I'm moving home and I don't know what that means for us." I sit down on the floor in front of the coffee table and open up a candy bar with a protein bar label… they're one in the same these days. I take a huge bite and talk with my mouth full. "Like, we only hooked up a week ago. Or two since we kissed I guess." I swallow. "But it's not serious enough to think he'd want to do long distance."

"Do you want to do long distance?"

"Whoa, getting right to the point are we?"

"It's easier this way." Nora says while handing me the bottle of wine. I take a sip but it burns going down.

"I don't know if I want to do long distance. Our connection is so strong when we're together. It almost feels easier to just end it now instead of delaying the inevitable."

"I guess that makes sense, it sucks, because you two are seriously cute, but I guess I get it."

"Up and at-em sailor!"

Nora's voice is chipper. Too chipper. She was at my side all night for the first bottle of wine, the second, the burrito, the nap, the club, and the second burrito.

"Whhhyyy?" I whine, "Why do I have to get up? I have no job, don't know what to do about my maybe boyfriend, and since I haven't paid off my credit card I don't even own these… sweats I don't remember buying." I say slowly as I look down at the very cute cream colored matching sweatpants and shirt I have on.

"They're my sweats."

"Oh, that's good I guess."

"But, your life does totally suck." I give her a look that borders on murderous but she just laughs in my face. "C'mon. It's a summer Saturday and we have options. I'm not going to allow you to wallow away in self pity while I only have a week left with you in the city."

"Uuuugh, fine. Hand me a bagel and tell me the options."

Nora beams because I've caved so easily, who has the energy to fight anyways. She bounces back into the room with a sesame, toasted, and sits criss-cross applesauce on the bed.

"O.K." She sounds like a cheerleader. Which is encouraging and annoying at the same time. "Option 1 is to go to the beach and lay on a towel all day and read a book. Option 2," she's ticking the list off on her fingers, "is to head to an indoor trampoline park and spend the afternoon bouncing around. No one can be sad while bouncing."

"That sounds like a workout." I say while my stomach does a somersault.

"Which could be good for you. But there's one more option." She clears her throat, I wait for her to ask for a drumroll please but she doesn't. "Option 3 is to spend the day in our dressiest clothes going in and out of art galleries pretending to be lesbian art connoisseurs."

"HA! Ohmigod that one. Obviously I want to do Option 3. I need a day to pretend to be someone else."

"I figured. Okay, are we going as fancy woodsy lesbians or sleek big city power house lesbians?"

"Sleek big city power with a hint of Holly Golightly."

Nora nods and takes a sip of her iced coffee. I can tell she's got more on her mind.

"What about Kyle?" She asks not making eye contact with me but picking at the elastic in her socks instead.

"What *about* Kyle?"

"Well he called again last night while you were showering before we went out. I didn't answer because I don't know where your head is at. And I was excited that I convinced you to go out. I didn't want you getting sad again and staying in." She starts to pick at something on her comforter. Feelings really are difficult for her to get out. "I just gotta ask this, get it out. Why couldn't you move in with him?"

"We haven't talked about it."

"Does he know you're leaving?"

"Yes, he knows I'm leaving. I think he does at least." Did I tell him on the phone yesterday? I can't remember. "But either way, he doesn't have a salary for me to start collecting, there's nothing he can do."

"Has he offered to have you move in? I could totally see him doing that."

"No. We've been dating for like a week. That'd be crazy." Although if he asked I would pause to seriously consider it. I didn't move to the city to become a live-in girlfriend but being at his place this past week has been amazing. We fell in step together naturally. But there's no way he'd consider asking me to move in. "It would be way too soon for me to move in with him."

"Fine. Finish that bagel and get in the shower."

"Yes sir."

CHAPTER 33

KYLE

Liz never called me back last night. No texts. Nothing. I spent the night pacing my apartment. I finally got to sleep in the early hours of the morning but I woke up this morning and still hadn't heard from her. I called again and it went straight to voicemail.

I didn't bother leaving a message.

She doesn't want to talk to me, that much I understand. What I don't understand is why. Why doesn't she want to see me? Talk this through with me? Figure something out?

Is she going to move home? Is she going to try and find a job? Stay with Nora for a while? Hell, she could move in with me. If she was talking to me at the moment I'd suggest it but I have a feeling if I showed up at Nora's with a spare set of keys she'd go running for the hills.

We hadn't made specific plans for today but in the back of my mind I expected us to spend it together. To do what we did last weekend. Simply be together. It felt so natural, so right. I don't think I can do the things I would normally do on a Saturday without her now. If I'm not going to do chores what can I do?

And this is the moment I realize that I have no on-demand hobbies. The band sets are scheduled, softball games, scheduled, tee times, scheduled. Running isn't officially scheduled but I do follow a routine.

I guess I could go for a run.

I already stress-cleaned my apartment last night. I check the fridge and I have enough groceries. There are a few economics books on my shelf but I'm not really in the mood.

Okay, fine, I'll go for a run.

Yeah, running was a good idea. My feet are light as I finish the loop through the park I always take and head towards my apartment. There's something about running that sets my mind at ease. It becomes this blank slate. Sometimes I have good ideas and come home and try to get everything down on paper and other times my mind just goes blank.

Today all I'm doing is running through the events of yesterday.

After turning down the offer from Fosters I went back to the conference room, dropped my badge on the table, grabbed my backpack, and high tailed it out of there. If Nora got an offer and I got an offer that means Liz didn't. I started calling her as soon as I got to the sidewalk.

What I don't understand is why she would hang out with Nora, who not only got an offer but accepted it, and she won't talk to me who turned it down.

I gave up on calling Liz for a minute last night and called my aunt instead. We talked over when I would officially start, Monday, and what she's already done to organize the camp project. She mentioned that I'll be paired with a more experienced project manager at the start to help get everything organized. I told her I appreciated that because I'm not sure what experience I actually got from Fosters.

Although, I can say I didn't need experience to know that the way Fosters offered me the job was backwards. They praised my work. My connections. Then put down Liz for not being as polished.

They discounted her because of her lack of finesse when in reality they had kept such a tight rein on everything she did that she spent her internship being worried she'd put a step wrong. I knew the job wasn't right for me from the start and I honestly don't think the job is right for Liz either.

She's too smart for them. They want someone who can just do what they're told but Liz thinks too much to just follow directions. And sure, she's not buttoned up and professional all the time but she is charismatic, kind, and funny.

Thinking of Liz puts a smile on my face. It's a beautiful day and I'm feeling energized so I turn south and kind of wind my way around the side streets at a slower pace. Eventually it's barely a jog and I realize that I am just walking around New York City for maybe the first time ever.

I have nowhere to go. I have no one I'm meeting. I'm just strolling. On the block ahead there are two women coming out of a gallery, giggling. They're dressed to the nines and usually I don't notice things like that but one has the cutest ass I've seen since -

Wait.

It is Liz.

Liz and Nora are stumbling down the street and it's obvious they're tipsy.

I watch as they make their way to the corner. Nora pulls out her phone. I managed to cross the street without them noticing me and as I approach them, I muster my deepest, police officer-esc voice and say, "Excuse me ma'ams."

Nora jumps backwards, throws her phone in the air, and squeals while Liz manages to wheel around and whack me with her purse. And by the feel of it she's got a brick in it.

"Oh shit!" Liz says as she spins back towards Nora.

"Ohmygosh KYLE! I thought you were a cop!" Nora yells as Liz helps her straighten out.

"Ha yeah, that was the point." I rub my arm where her purse made contact. "What are you two doing?"

They glance at each other and have an entire conversation with their eyes. From what I can gather they're saying 'I'm not going to be the one to tell him - you are.'

Finally Liz caves. She takes a deep breath.

"Okay, so this is embarrassing." Liz starts, swaying slightly.

"It can't be that bad." I try to hide my laughter.

"We're playing pretend." Nora says flatly.

"Shut up! I was going to tell him. Gosh you can't keep your mouth shut when you are tipsy!" Liz turns to me, squares her shoulders, clears her throat, and continues.

"After I didn't get the job yesterday, Nora took me home, we had a bottles of wine and then went out all night. Today Nora kindly offered to play pretend with me."

"What?" I'm both amused and confused.

"Well since I've got nothing going for me in the life department I've got five days to live it up big time city style before I go home."

"Home to Lakeville?" She can't. She won't. I know we just started dating but I can't imagine my daily routines without her anymore.

"Yep." Sadness crosses through her eyes before she steels herself.

"Where does playing pretend come into it?" I ask. I am not going to force the conversation about her moving home. I definitely don't want to have it in front of Nora.

"Well, it's simple. Sometimes it is easier to ignore problems like rent and job hunting and the shambles of your life in general don't exist by pretending to be lesbian art buyers to get free booze from galleries in the middle of the day."

A guffaw of a laugh escapes me. That is just such a ridiculous thing that honestly only these two could come up with. "You guys are insane."

"And proud of it." Nora adds with a hiccup.

A black car comes around the corner. The driver gets out of the front seat, looks at Nora.

"Pick up for Nora Heely?"

"Righto govnah!" Nora says with a salute.

"Ohmigosh," Liz says with a mirthful laugh. "Get her in the car."

And naturally I pile in with them.

CHAPTER 34

LIZ

Was it embarrassing to have Kyle run into Nora and I playing pretend? Yes.

Is this just my M.O. now?

Apparently.

Falling down and doing dumb shit in front of the boy I like.

Why not.

Just add it to the pity pile I'll be packing up this week to take home.

Kyle came back with us to Nora's. She was donezo so I helped her change into PJs and get tucked into bed. I sobered up the minute I saw him on the sidewalk outside the gallery. Cold dose of reality. Now that Nora is tucked in, we are sitting on her sofa close to each other but not close enough to be touching.

There is absolutely an elephant in the room and we both know it. We are both staring right at it. If I'm lucky it'll start the conversation and mediate between Kyle and I. The idea makes me chuckle.

"What?" Kyle asks, looking at me.

Guess I chuckled out loud. And I guess I might not be as sober as I thought I was because what I say is "I'm waiting for the elephant to start talking."

The look Kyle gives me is one of concern. He probably thinks I have a head injury.

"No." I let out another laugh. "Okay, how to explain? I was thinking that me moving home is a giant elephant in the room and then I pictured both of us looking at it and starting a conversation to get us to talk about our feelings."

"That is kind of funny." He says without a hint of mirth.

More silence. It is so incredibly awkward. I already know he's going to be sensitive to my feelings. And I should be sensitive to his feelings too but I'm the one who is losing more here. My whole life trajectory changed yesterday in the matter of a 10 minute meeting. His life is chugging along according to plan. I take a bracing breath and pivot towards him on the sofa. Tucking my knees up into my chest and hugging them.

"Alright, here's the deal." He looks at me and there is pain in his beautiful blue eyes. My mind draws a blank for a split second. Do I have to do this? Can't I just keep pretending to be Dolores Nightingale lesbian art collector?

No?

I can't?

Fine.

"I called my parents yesterday and they're going to come and pick me up on Thursday and I'm moving home."

"You've already decided?"

"Yeah, I don't have any other options. I was going to go home anyway for Float Fest but now instead of taking the train my parents are going to come and help me move out."

I look back up at him and immediately I feel tears well in my eyes. My nose stings. I need to break this tension, to find something else to talk about.

"Get me pizza." Nora calls out from her room. I laugh because she must have sensed my discomfort and need for a distraction. Good friend that she is.

"You got it, girlfriend." I call back. I look at Kyle and he smiles but it doesn't reach his eyes.

Thirty minutes later we are huddled around Nora's coffee table enjoying slices. Nora's gaze is ping-ponging back and forth between Kyle and me. I can see her wheels turning. And I don't like it.

"So why don't you just move in with Kyle again?"

I glare at Nora and I feel Kyle's gaze snap to my face.

"Because that's not an option *Nora*. And it's none of your business."

"Fine, but how are you supposed to get a job in the city if you're all the way up in Lakeville?"

"I'm not." I say with a shrug. If I try to be casual about it maybe it won't feel like such a crushing blow.

"Couldn't you stay here and do photography full-time?" Kyle asks while he wipes his mouth.

"What photography?" Nora asks, looking between us again.

"The stock photography stuff. Like what I did at Chandler's parent's place."

"Oh yeaaah, that stuff was cool. You sell it right?"

"She does, and she sells a lot of it." Kyle chimes in for me. His unwavering support with the photography work always surprises me. There is zero doubt in his mind about it.

"I wouldn't have to worry about a code of conduct if I was my own boss." I say with a laugh but as soon as I say it out loud, it seems reasonable.

"It's seriously such bull shit that they didn't give you the job for *business decorum*." Nora says. "I don't know what it was like to work with Marcus and Lauren but the Education team is a lot more laid back. Definitely a tenured professor vibe in that department."

I can't remember what I told Kyle about not getting the job. I guess it's all coming out now. Another tally in my embarrassing moments in front of the boyfriend column.

"So wait, what happened in your meeting?" Kyle sets down his pizza and gives me his full attention.

"Basically, they pulled me in, said I wasn't polished enough for the job, and told me to go." I'm talking to my knees at this point because I can't lift my head to look at Kyle. He knows how hard I worked this summer. How much I wanted it. And now he knows that I fell short.

That I wasn't good enough.

"No way." Kyle, to his credit, does look surprised but now that I've had a day to digest it I can totally see where they're coming from. My clothes weren't the most polished, my hair never really cooperated. I did make some mistakes and I got too caught up in doing the data visualization parts of the projects that other tasks were neglected. And I was clumsy. For their firm who runs on reputation I wouldn't be a good representative.

"It's fine. I mean, it isn't but, it is what it is." Again I shrug. I need a change of topic. "Who wants ice cream?"

Nora, to my delight, raises her hand and jumps up. She grabs her purse and heads straight to the door.

"I also want wine."

CHAPTER 35

LIZ

It was weird not to go to work today. Like the rest of the city got up and dressed and went to their job and I just sat there on the sofa in my PJs sipping coffee and staring at my laptop. After ice cream, Kyle and I walked Nora home and then he asked me to come back to his place with him. I stayed the night and on Sunday we walked, and talked, and ate, and took a nap. After dinner he walked me home and kissed me goodnight at my door. Fifteen minutes later he texted me good night when he got home and it put a big smile on my face.

But today, without anything to do, I'm lost. Half of me wants to curl back up in bed and try again tomorrow. The other half of me wants to be a boss ass bitch and apply to jobs. And all weekend Kyle got me thinking about being a photographer.

Maybe I'll use today to create a website for myself?

Gosh, what would my dad say if I told him I was a professional photographer?

Probably something about savings accounts.

Or health insurance.

The reality is that I would still have to move home because of the whole rent and cost of living situation.

I get myself dressed, grab my photography stuff and drop my phone in my purse. From somewhere in the depths my phone pings with a text.

KYLE: Good Morning! How's your first day of Funemployment going?

LIZ: Ha. I'm gonna use that! It's fine. Just trying to figure out where to start.

KYLE: Where do you want to start?

LIZ: Well, if you must know. I'm headed out the door in a minute in jean shorts, on a freaking Monday, like a college student, and I'm headed to the cafe for a coffee, pastry, and pictures.

KYLE: Nice! What cafe?

LIZ: Collectiva

KYLE: That's a good one. If I wasn't working a whole borough away I'd come join you.

LIZ: Too bad :(

KYLE: Wanna come over for dinner instead?

LIZ: Oooo, that was smooth!

LIZ: Yeah, let's have dinner. What do you say to pancakes?

KYLE: One of the three things I know how to cook!

LIZ: Wow! Three whole things!

KYLE: You got the pasta already, pancakes tonight. That's one and two. Number three is…

LIZ: No wait! Let me guess! Grilled Chicken.

KYLE: Nope. But I can cook that so four things.

LIZ: Mac N Cheese

KYLE: Nope, I'd classify that under Pasta

LIZ: Ah I see, so there are like parent categories.

KYLE: Most definitely.

LIZ: Then the third thing you know how to make is - drumroll please - Sandwiches.

KYLE: Yes! Nailed it.

KYLE: And this is a diverse category. Sandwiches include grilled cheese, turkey, BLT, PB&J, and cucumber. I'm really good at putting things between bread.

LIZ: Why does that sound like innuendo?

KYLE: Because you have the brain of a 15 year old boy.

LIZ: Facts.

KYLE: Okay, pancakes, my place. Does 7 work?

LIZ: SLAP - sounds like a plan.

The coffee shop at 10am on a Monday is a very different vibe than at 7:35 when I am running late but need caffeine. First of all, there's no line. It confused me at first and I thought maybe they were closed but the kid behind the counter in a cap and apron scrolling on his phone is clearly here to make me coffee. He doesn't look like a latte art aficionado so I'm gonna skip the lattes for today's photos. One of the two tables up front by the window will be perfect. I order my hot coffee for here and an iced coffee to go, yes this confuses the kid but I need them in those cups for photos, and a croissant for here. Then I ask for a to go pastry bag.

Poor kid doesn't know what to make of me.

Not worth the effort to try and explain it to him.

I take my items over to the front table and begin to set up. First I take a couple of test shots to judge the lighting and the settings. Once I'm happy with it I reach for my prop pouch filled with, earbuds, a notebook, pens, and hair clips. I also have in my bag keys, lip glosses, crumpled receipts and mints. There is a man behind me at a table with his laptop out and big over the ear noise canceling headphones. I bend down to get his attention which he gives me quickly, impatiently, so I motion to the chair, smile, shrug my shoulders and nod towards my table. His reply is the smallest of nods before returning to his screen.

I use this second chair as my prop table. Since the iced coffee is what I want to drink and the cup will start sweating soon I start with it, the pastry bag, earbuds, and my keys. A "gather up before going to the door" shot. I arrange the items, step back, and shoot.

Rearrange, step back, and shoot.

Rearrange, step back, and shoot.

I turn to the other side of the table for the next shots, I'm going to try and capture the shot in a bokeh background look. Headphones is looking at me. I give him a quick smile and get back to my shot. I stand up tall and look at the preview screen on the back of the camera when I notice Headphones has started packing up his bag. He doesn't seem thrilled so I resist the urge to ask if I can take some photos of him doing it. He doesn't seem like the type who would smile and say "oh sure!"

Once he leaves I swap out the accessories and put the croissant on the table. My stomach rumbles so I decide to shoot one quickly and then I rip the croissant in half and take a bite. Half is good enough for a picture right? Makes it seem more relatable? I might as well have some of the iced coffee too.

I swap out more props with the hot coffee cup and these look more corporate. I'm in my rearrange, step back, and shoot routine when someone comes up to sit at the table vacated by Headphones. I look up and see a nanny and small kid. The kid is in the stroller but clearly wants out. I feel ya, kid.

I turn my back to them and, you guessed it, rearrange, step back, and shoot when the toddler reaches up and pulls on the coffee mug, sending thankfully no longer hot coffee all over the table.

"Louis! No!" The nanny scolds. The kid starts crying. "I'm so sorry, miss." She says to me.

I smile, "It's fine" and the nanny hands me some napkins. I'm reaching over for them when the kid climbs up in the chair at my table with a car in his chubby little hand. He starts to drive the car around the table avoiding the lake of coffee that has settled. My camera is still poised so I click a shot of the table with his hand driving the little toy around Lake Coffee.

The nanny pulls little Louis back to the stroller and buckles him in which he does *not* like. Her coffee is not in a to go cup, clearly she planned to hang out here for a minute. She begins the process of calming him down and I'm surprised when it works. She's sweetly singing to him and his eyes are transfixed on her. From my point of view Elmo himself could walk into the coffee shop and he wouldn't notice. I don't even feel myself thinking about it before I snap a picture of the two of them.

I turn back to my table. Clean up and decide to pack up. Maybe I'll grab lunch on the way home. Sometimes when I get so caught up in what I'm doing I forget to eat. This morning felt like that. It must be like three in the afternoon or something.

I pull my phone out of my pocket.

Nope. It's 10:35.

So not lunch time yet.

CHAPTER 36

KYLE

My first day at YouthFull was awesome. After a summer at Fosters I figured any other office would be better but YF exceeded my expectations. Everyone was friendly and helpful and they already had a jump start on the logistics of securing a camp location. We had a brainstorming session all afternoon about the programs we would offer, the potential challenges we would face, and the solutions to those challenges.

The annual board meeting starts on Monday and we are presenting the camp proposal to the board for approval. We need financials, programming, insurance, and staffing requirements all mapped out. It's a lot to do in a few days. But I am energized and the team is too.

And if a fulfilling day of work wasn't enough I now get to go and make pancakes for Liz. I'm excited to hear about her day. Tell her about mine. My body warms as I envision us sharing the night together.

I enjoyed seeing her every day at Fosters this summer and you'd think that last week when we got to see each other all day and all night it would be too much but it wasn't. I can't get enough of her.

We never run out of things to say or share.

Except we can't seem to talk about what to do when she moves home.

In four days her dad is coming to pack up her stuff and drive her home.

Four days.

Any chance my brain gets to engage in an internal debate it does. On one hand, I don't want to be with anyone else. On the other, I don't want to date long distance.

It's not that far to Lakeville but can our relationship survive on weekend visits? I like her so much that I want to say yes. That we'd find a way.

But, we're in the almost-constant-sex phase of this relationship and you can't go straight to only texts and twice a month IRL visits from there.

The other thing is she hasn't really brought it up to me yet. She doesn't seem to be considering staying in the city at all. Maybe she's trying to let me down easy. Protect me from a brutal breakup. Or maybe she's in denial. Either way, we need to talk about what is happening after this week. The stress of not talking about it has got to be worse than just getting it all out there.

Rip off the bandage as they say.

I change into a pair of gym shorts when I get home and I'm about to grab a t-shirt when I hear a knock at the door. Knowing Liz will appreciate me with my shirt off I open the door with a sly grin on my face.

That grin disappears when I see Liz standing there with a sad sort of smile on her face and then I realize she's leaning on crutches.

"What happened!?" I ask as she hobbles past me to the sofa.

"I sprained my ankle," she says with a sigh as she positions her crutches on the arm of the sofa and hops around to take a seat. When she flops down the crutches she has balanced just a moment before, go sliding to the ground.

"Shit," she mutters and she goes to reach them but I get them for her. As I stand them back up I can see the tears in her eyes.

"Liz, hey, it's okay, things happen." I say as I take a seat on the coffee table in front of her.

"You'd be proud though, I remembered RICE."

"I'm not hungry." I reply and all she can muster is a small huff of a laugh. "So, what kind of trouble did you get into today?"

"I was walking home from the coffee shop this morning. Which was a really productive little session, and I decided to meander through the park. I ended up taking a bunch of photos of the full scene. I don't know what the term is but it wasn't one particular detail or an overhead shot, it was like a point of view of the busy park. Does that make sense?"

I nod so she continues.

"There was a walking taco truck at the end of the park so I stopped and grabbed one."

"Who wouldn't?" She smiles at my comment.

"Right? Irresistible. Anyways I was carrying lunch in one hand and still had my camera slung over my arm so I picked it up with the other hand and started to take a few pictures of the walking taco. I wasn't watching where I was going and my next step was half on and half off the curb. I felt my ankle pop to the side and it hurt really bad right away. I wasn't too far from home so I hobbled as best I could. It had swelled up a bunch by the time I got home. I got some frozen veggies on it and elevated it and for whatever reason my roommate had these crutches so I'm using them."

"How is it feeling now?"

"Sore." She shrugs again and looks down at her ankle. I take a pillow from my bed and prop it under her foot so it's elevated even more.

"Still want pancakes?"

"Yeah."

The pancakes seem to cheer Liz up. She's much more chatty now. We talked all about my first day and the plans for the camp. She described some of the photos she took.

We have not talked about her leaving on Thursday.

I feel like it's now or never.

"Do you have a lot to do before Thursday?" I ask from the sink where I'm washing out the pan. Feeling like a chicken because I can't be face to face with her for this conversation.

"Nah, I didn't have much with me to begin with so it's mostly clothes. But it'll be nice to have a laundry service."

"What do you mean?" I didn't think Liz's parents were struggling but I also didn't think they had like maids and stuff.

"My mom will insist on doing my laundry. I don't understand the woman but she loves doing laundry. She'll be excited to have a new bundle to add to the rotation."

"Rotation?"

"Oh yes, she has a system. Sunday, sheets. Monday, towels. Tuesday, her clothes. Wednesday, Dad's clothes. Thursday was my clothes, now I think she does towels again. She now takes Fridays and Saturdays off. The rotation changed when my older siblings left for college but she used to do a load a day."

"Ha, that is a system. Did she teach you the tiny folding method?"

"She did but late night organized closet video binges made me a master. She's gonna have trouble with my thongs."

I cough from my surprise. Liz catches my eye and the sparkle has returned. I have a feeling that if I ask her again about what we do when she moves home that sparkle will disappear.

"What are your plans tomorrow?" I ask her instead. One day at a time.

"Nora was going to take me out for a night of fun but now with this," she motions to her ankle, "I'm not sure. Maybe just dinner with her or something. Why?"

"Just curious. If you've got plans tomorrow, can we do dinner on Wednesday? I'll take you out to that sushi place Chandler loves."

"Ooo yes! That sounds perfect."

We settle in on the sofa together. I slide in under the pillow propping her leg up and place my hands on her shins. I have to resist the urge to glide the backs of my fingers up to her knee and beyond. I'm assuming she doesn't want to start anything up at the moment since she's nursing a sprained ankle but I'm on borrowed time.

CHAPTER 37

LIZ

"Yes, I do want to keep watching, thankyouverymuch." I say outloud to the TV as I reach for the remote. The sushi was delivered three episodes ago. I started eating my half about halfway through the second episode. I grab a roll from Kyle's half now because it's sitting there.

He sounded stressed and regretful when he called to ask if it was OK to stay in because he wasn't going to make it to our 7:30 reservation. I said it was fine and that I was excited to see him either way and then shuffled back to my spot on the sofa. I didn't bother changing out of the yellow dress that I had dug out of my box of clothes and steamed in the bathroom while I took a shower.

For the record it kind of helped but there are still some creases in it.

They're worse now that I've been crumpled on the sofa for the last, checks phone, two and a half hours.

I know I need to talk to him about how I'm feeling. Share that I've never felt this way about a guy, boy, man, ugh, any person, before and that if I wasn't moving home I would be all about a serious relationship.

That I'm falling in love with him.

I've already fallen for him.

But I just can't picture us being together when I've moved away. I know I poo-pooed his idea of moving in with him when Nora suggested it on his behalf. Honestly all I kept thinking about was how devastating it would be to move out of his place someday when we broke up. I just could not move in with him now, live with him, fall even more in love with him, and then move out later. That would be more heartbreaking than ending things now. And I am NOT expecting him to follow me or anything silly like that. When I look back some day I'll see this is a super intense summer fling. But actually telling him it's over will only make this whole thing harder.

That's what she said.

Oh god, I'm losing my mind.

This YouthFull camp is so huge for him. It is exciting that he was able to hit the ground running with his team right away. From what he told me on Monday night they already have a location they're interested in and today they were having meetings with insurance companies. I don't want to distract him from this project. And while our relationship feels all consuming right now, I don't ever want to feel like I come second to his work or feel like he's sacrificing work for me.

I know that's a contradiction but I believe healthy couples find a way to have career success and relationship success. He's finding his career success and I'm about to add Couch Potato to my LinkedIn.

I haven't picked up my camera or laptop to edit photos since Monday. I got home and packed it up after icing my ankle. The desire to create a website for myself is gone. The belief that being a photographer is possible is gone too. I'll go home, work at the coffee shop or something, and keep applying for jobs everywhere I can.

It's on me to make this career happen. No one is going to hand it to me.

My phone pings with a text.

I reach for it incredibly quickly and twinge a muscle in my side.

Shit that hurts.

DAD: Excited to pick you up tomorrow kiddo! I'll be there at 10:30 so we can pack up and beat all the traffic out of the city.

LIZ: Sounds like a plan Dad. See you tomorrow.

Now that my phone is in my hand I decide I'll just do it. I'll text Kyle.

LIZ: Hey, any ETA yet?

KYLE: A few issues came up. My guess is another hour of work so like 10:30

LIZ: Okay, see you then. Just let yourself in.

I'm ticked. I set my phone face down on the sofa like I'm giving it a time out and try to get lost in the TV but I can't shake the disappointment that my phone is sitting next to me on the sofa and not Kyle.

And it doesn't take long for me to get really pissed from there. It's my last night in the city. The proposal isn't even due until Monday! I don't know how much he has left to do or what his insurance meetings mean but he could work all night *tomorrow* but he's doing it tonight.

Shucks, I might have been waiting for a grand gesture.

The fact that he hasn't surprised me with one proves I'm right not to bring up my feelings for him. It'll be easier to just pile on the lost potential of a relationship with Kyle to the pity party pile waiting for me in my childhood bedroom at home.

I wake up with a start on the sofa. This time, no, I don't want to keep watching.

My phone confirms the time, 1:30 in the morning. The sushi is still sitting out and there's no sign of Kyle.

I get up and get ready for bed. I'm climbing in ten minutes later and plugging in my phone to charge when a text comes in.

KYLE: Liz, I am so sorry. We're just finishing up now and I'm sure you're already in bed so I'm going to head home. I'll stop by in the morning with coffee. Night.

I take a deep breath and shoot off a quick text before setting my phone to DO NOT DISTURB.

CHAPTER 38

KYLE

I'm knocking on Liz's door at 7:15am with two iced coffees and bagels. It is early for Liz but with it being her moving day I'm expecting her to be up.

There's no answer so I knock again.

There are finally sounds behind the door and I remember she might not be moving quickly with her ankle and feel back that I knocked twice.

I'm anxious to see her I guess.

But instead of seeing Liz's face when the door opens it's her roommate.

"What's up?" She drolls.

"Umm, is Liz here?" I ask while trying to peer around her shoulders to see into the apartment.

"Nah man, she's already gone."

I'm too surprised to respond so the roommate just shrugs and closes the door.

After a beat the door reopens and I'm expecting Liz to be yelling at her roommate for being such a dope but instead it's the roommate again and she reaches out and takes a coffee and the bagel bag before closing the door again.

Fuck. What do I do now?

January 1 | 9:24am

Hey Kyle,

I'm chickening out and emailing you instead of texting or calling or facetiming. I've gotten all of yours and I'm sorry that I couldn't muster the courage to respond. I was too hurt. Am too hurt. The pain I woke up with every morning has faded since August and I've had the time and space to do a lot of thinking in the last several months.

I don't blame you but a part of me is glad to have the way I spent my last night in the city as a reason things ended between us. This past summer spent with you is one I'll never forget.

Now that we've got 100 miles, and a few months of cold turkey, between us, let's be friends, yeah? I think that's what I miss the most. I miss my friend Kyle.

Let's see. I've been home for four months and there are some updates to share.

Float Fest was a lot of fun. Glad that it happened the weekend I got home because it served as a distraction. I ended up falling into the water while trying to catch a football - which I'm sure you're not surprised by at all - and one of my crutches fell overboard and sunk.

Speaking of which, the ole ankle is A-OK. Thank you for teaching me R.I.C.E. I have a feeling it'll come in handy.

My mom is happily doing my laundry, but she brings it up in the basket to my room for me to fold and put away. I guess adult children don't get full-service laundry at the Collins B&B.

I started working at the coffee shop in town and I am still taking photos - I knew you'd ask.

A few photos of us are attached. I had edited them back in the city but never got around to sharing them with you and then couldn't bear to open the folder until today. Maybe it's the foot of snow outside but the images make me feel all warm and fuzzy. That was such a fun day. Remember when the squirrel snatched a fry off the table! I don't know if you or I screamed louder.

Good times.

Okay, I'm going to go join my parents for dinner and Jeopardy.
Happy New Year,
Take care - Liz

January 1 | 9:57 am

Liz, Hi,

Thank you for your email. I figured my texts and calls were too much at the time but I hate the way we ended things. There was no closure. You were just gone. I think about you all the time.

I'm trying not to be too lovesick over you but that's what I'm feeling at the moment. The days aren't as bright without you. The nights are not as warm. The small moments we had together were everything and I miss them so much. Miss you so much.

Thank you for sending those pictures. I remember that day and the way you couldn't keep the smile off your face, especially when reenacting the fry robbery. That squirrel is a menace to society and should be arrested. I don't eat outside anymore because of him.

I'm glad to hear that you're making a routine for yourself in Lakeville. I'm sure the whole town is glad to have Liz Collins back because the city certainly misses you.

Things with the camp are coming along fine. The board did approve it so we're busy trying to get things organized to open camp next summer.

I'm still playing music with Jeff and Chris once a month at Coopers. We've found a few times to practice in between sets together too which has been a fun way to fill the time since you left. Not sure if you've kept up with Chandler but he landed a job with the NY Rovers hockey team charity. I'm going to a game with him in a few weeks.

I regret that we didn't get to see each other that night. I regret that I didn't leave work sooner. I said it in all my texts and I'll say it again, I'm sorry.

Keep taking pictures, share them with me if you want. I'd love to see them.

Happy New Year to you too
Love, Kyle

CHAPTER 39

LIZ

"Here you go! Enjoy your day!"

The last of the morning rush is gone and I take a deep breath. Granted, the Lakeville morning rush is like eight regulars but they all come at the same time and then hang out and chat so it feels a lot busier than it is on paper. It took me a minute to get used to the slower pace again but after almost a year I've settled back in.

I pour myself an iced coffee, grab my laptop, and open it up to the photo I was editing last night.

It's a photo of the coffee shop from a few days ago. I take a picture on the third Friday of the month at noon to capture the front of the store as the seasons change. Each time I take one I remember the first one that I took.

It was the day after I got home.

The day after I chickened out from telling Kyle that I think I was falling in love with him.

Ten months later the emotions of that early morning when my dad arrived and packed up my few boxes in the matter of an hour always resurface when I take and edit this photo. But they're not quite as crippling as they were at the beginning.

I guess time does heal all wounds.

My New York City coffee drinking expertise came in handy when I talked to Mitchell about a job at his coffee shop downtown. We've added some flavor syrups and dairy alternative options. There's a partnership with the local bakery too.

His wife Sandy saw me editing the photo of the toddler playing near the spilled coffee and the one I took of him and his nanny. She gushed over them, I'm not sure why, and asked if I would display them at the shop. I got them printed on large canvases and she made a notecard next to it to display my name and email address.

Within a few days I had gotten four emails from moms around Lakeville wondering how much I charge for a family portrait session. I took the time to research what other photographers charge for family portraits and set something I felt was reasonable.

All four families booked with me and I had a lot of fun with the sessions. There was no part of the process that felt like a grind. From helping them select a location, to shooting them and capturing the love they share, to editing and sending them the final images. I was energized each step of the way.

I hadn't realized until then how much energy I put into my work at Fosters just to do the work. I was constantly telling myself to focus. To stay on track.

I emailed Kyle in January with some photos I had taken when we were together. The city was sparkling in those photos and the day held such positive memories. Stolen kisses (and fries), ice cream, and smiles. After several months of wallowing, and my own bottle of champagne on new years eve, I realized that it was time to reframe last summer in my mind. It was time to be grateful that it happened. That I had those experiences. That I knew what it felt to love another person in that way.

I realized that I had been a coward. I bailed. I told myself I was angry but really I was just trying to protect myself from the hurt that was already taking hold. I wouldn't say that I've completely dealt with these feelings. But, it is tough to wallow when you're busy serving coffee all morning, caught up in creative pursuits in the afternoons, and sitting with your chatty parents at dinner in the evenings.

I facetime with Nora every Monday night. She is still killing it at Fosters and seems to find a new guy each weekend. One and done seems to be her motto.

I'm at the point in photo editing where I can't tell if I'm done and that usually means I am. Better to leave it than over do it. I click over to my inbox and at the top is an email from Kyle. Subject line "Here".

Liz,

From the first day I saw you I knew you were special.

I know we haven't seen each other since last year but I'm convinced that you're the person I'm meant to spend my life with. I failed to tell you all the things that I needed to last summer.

Things you deserve to hear.

So, I'm here.

Talk soon,

Kyle

I look up from my screen with teary eyes.

The cafe is empty, no one is sitting at the table out front on the sidewalk. Part of me thought that maybe he'd be like standing outside of the cafe when I looked up but that's something that would only happen in a book or a movie so I'm actually glad he isn't. Makes it feel more real.

The tears are rolling down my face now and I don't want to be a sobbing mess if someone comes in so I grab my laptop and head to the kitchen in the back.

My mind is racing.

He thinks I'm his person.

I want to be his person.

It has felt like half of me is missing this past year, even while the whole of me has felt more settled than ever.

I get myself a glass of water, the tears are still streaming down my face. Relief may be the main emotion I'm feeling.

What do I do now? How do I respond? Should I call him? I'll have to wait until I stop crying because I'll sound like a goopy mess if I call now. I gulp down half the water when the bells on the front door jingles announcing someone's arrival.

"Just a minute!" I holler from the back before sniffling and shaking out my hands.

"I can wait."

Kyle.

He's *here*.

I round the corner from the back more quickly than I had planned and knock my shoulder into the door jam.

"Oh ow!" I exclaim as I right myself and look up. Kyle is crossing the cafe.

"You okay?" He says as he reaches me.

"Yeah," I whisper, "you're *here*."

He shrugs "I'm here."

CHAPTER 40

KYLE

She's speechless. She's stunned. I saw the hopeful look in her eye from my spot outside just past her line of vision when she finished reading the email. I expected her to walk outside to find me standing on the sidewalk.

When I saw her get up and rush to the back of the shop I had to move fast but now that she's in front of me I'm experiencing so many different feelings at once I'm not sure what to focus on first.

Relief. I decide to go with relief.

"How are you here?" She asks with disbelief.

"Well I got my car out of the lot, put my bag in the back seat and drove u—ooof!"

Liz cuts off my snarky reply by jumping into my arms. I squeeze her tight before I pull my head back and kiss her like it is my last day on earth. Our lips know exactly what to do and we quickly deepen the kiss with our tongues pressing into each other looking for maximum contact.

With one hand around her waist and the other cradling her beautiful face I feel like the wind has been knocked out of me. I pull away and rest my forehead on hers. The blood in my veins is pumping fast being connected with Liz again but at the same time things inside me feel steady, calm. Like the excitement is the icing on the cake to the feeling of just being near her again.

"Liz, I've been miserable without you. I have missed you every moment this last year. Every victory was shadowed and every disappointment heightened because you weren't there to share them with me."

Her head falls to my chest and she's either laughing or crying. I pull her chin up so she's looking at me and I realize it's both.

"Are these happy tears?"

"They're tears of relief I think. Kyle I'm so sorry for how I left. I've missed you too. And it's amazing that you're here. Unbelievable." I see a shadow pass through her eyes. She pulls back slightly, still in my arms. Her tone changes when she speaks again. "Why did you come? We're in the same boat as last summer."

"Not exactly the same boat." She looks confused and is about to speak when I cut her off by placing my finger to her lips. They're soft, warm, and wet from our exchange a moment ago. "What time do you close?"

"Two."

"Okay, I'll be back at two to pick you up."

"Promise?"

"Pinky promise," and I hold my pinky to her and she playfully links hers with mine.

The next two hours pass at a snail's pace. I walk through downtown Lakeville exploring the shops. There's a hardware store that doesn't look like it's changed since the 1940s and a bookstore devoted solely to romance called Tropes and Flings. I spend a decent amount of time in the outdoor goods and camping store but by 1:30 I just go and sit in my car outside the coffee shop.

Thirty minutes of scrolling and replying to a few work emails pass and I see her locking up the coffee shop. I get out of the car and open the passenger door for her.

"Oh wow. You're pulling out all the stops aren't you!" She says with a grin on her face. I also take her bag from her.

"I'm trying to woo you. Is it working?"

"Yes."

We both laugh and smile like goons at each other. I put her bag in the backseat and walk around to my side of the car. I climb in and pivot towards her. "Ready?" I ask.

"I guess so. I don't know what we're doing so I don't know if I'm ready?"

"Isn't that killing you?"

"Not as much as I would have thought. I must trust you." She says as she buckles up.

"Good."

It's a short drive to Camp. And Liz knows the roads so I don't have much time for this to remain a mystery.

"Okay, Kyle, level with me, what's going on? Why are you here, driving me around my hometown?"

"Do you really want me to tell you or do you want it to be a surprise?"

"I want you to tell me, I've got too wild an imagination for surprises."

"Ha, fair enough. Well…" we're turning on to Old Camp Road so I don't need to stretch this out much longer anyway, "As you know, YouthFull is opening a camp, but what you don't know is that it's happ-en-ing" I stretch the word out a second longer than needed as I make the final turn towards the entrance to the camp grounds, "here."

Liz is staring at me, unblinking. "What do you mean, 'here'?"

"YouthFull bought the camp. Well, a donor did and then gifted it to us. We've had a team in there fixing things up for a few months and it's looking like we can host our first campers in July. We're only doing a few weeks this first summer but I hope we can do a winter camp over school holidays and then do six or even eight weeks next summ…"

Liz has stepped out of the car and is walking towards the lodge. She turns back to me slowly.

"So, are you moving here for the next few weeks?" She asks.

"No."

CHAPTER 41

KYLE

And that's the crushing blow right there. The other shoe has dropped. He declares I'm his person, I fall right back in love. He is here now but he's not staying. I put two and two together when we turned onto Old Camp Road and tried not to get my hopes up.

I bring my eyes up to meet his from where I had been studying the dirt.

If he sees the disappointment on my face he doesn't show it because he's smiling.

"I'm here. Like, permanently."

What now?

I'm speechless again, twice in one day. New record.

"Aunt Mary agreed to let me be the camp director and to live up here permanently. I'll head back into the city every so often for meetings but I'll be living here."

"Oh. Wow. Okay. So. Sorry, I'm just trying to catch up."

"It's a lot I know." He laughs and walks over to take my hands in his. "After the camp was approved at the board meeting last year I could barely work on it. I was constantly reminded of how I'd hurt you. I spent the next month barely able to get myself out of bed. Every text I sent that went unanswered gutted me. Every call that went to voicemail broke my heart a little more. I knew that night that I was making a mistake, choosing to stay late at work over hanging out with you. But a part of me thought that maybe if I didn't see you then we wouldn't actually have to end things. That we'd just continue on. Man," he scoffs, "Was I wrong.

"Then you emailed me the photos of us together this summer and I knew what I wanted to do. What I had to do. YouthFull had already secured the camp property and I desperately wanted to tell you everything when I wrote back but I couldn't disappoint you again.

"In April I gave Aunt Mary the choice between me as camp director in Lakeville or me quitting all together. I needed the job for all the reasons, being outdoors, helping the kids and," he takes a deep breath and rolls his shoulders back, "And, that being camp director would bring me closer to you." He takes another deep breath.

"They agreed. And, well, here I am." He shrugs.

"Here you are." I say with a smile on my face as I squeeze his hands and lean in so our foreheads meet.

This is the best of both worlds. This is the big romantic gesture a girl hopes for even if it feels like it's ten months too late.

But also this delayed gesture makes me fall for him even more. I don't want to be less important than his work but I also don't want to get in the way. He got the job lined up because of me but before coming to me. And, while it was incredibly painful, the time apart allowed me to get my career and life established on my own. I have a successful photography business so we're both bringing ourselves and our careers to the table.

Knowing his grand gesture is well planned out and logical, and that the delay between last summer and now allowed me to flourish, butterflies have taken flight in my stomach and the sense of relief, happiness and, well, love I feel for him standing there is overwhelming.

"Liz? I can see the wheels turning. What's going through your mind?"

"Umm, everything. I'm surprised. I'm excited. I'm scared. I'm thrilled. I'm a little pissed if I'm being honest."

"Pissed? As pissed as I felt when your roommate took your bagel and iced coffee after telling me you were gone?"

"Probably." I drop his hands and cross my arms. Even though this is new information and I want to know more.

"Listen," he put his hands on his hips and takes a few steps away in a circle. "I didn't surprise you today to start a fight. I knew there was a chance you'd resent me. Really, Liz, I was telling the truth when I said that you're the person I want to spend my life with. I know we're going from zero to sixty and that you technically haven't said yes to anything but that kiss this morning tells me you might."

"Yeah, I might. But, you haven't really asked me anything yet."

"Oh." And he pulls on his ear lobe with embarrassment. He looks up, I can see his shoulders rise and fall with a deep breath. He crosses over to me in determined and swift steps.

"Well then, here goes nothing. Liz, will you be my person? Spend as much time with me as you can stand? Look at the stars with me? Make coffee with me in the mornings? Will you -"

"You're rambling," I whisper as I take a half step closer.

He takes my hands in his, brings them to his mouth and kisses them and whispers, "I do that when I'm nervous."

I smile as I pull one hand away to slide around his waist. He brings his arm around my shoulders and holds me. I look up at him from where I'm pressed against his chest. He leans down and kisses me and the ground seems to shake under my feet. It took us some time to get to this point. It took us being apart to know how much we need to be together.

"Don't be nervous. I'm here." I say with a smile.

EPILOGUE

LIZ

"I'm here! I'm here!" I yell as I sprint up the road to the camp's main parking lot. It is the last day of camp for the summer and Kyle has put together a successful three weeks.

He hired me as the art tent coordinator so I've been working with the kids on all sorts of projects. The classic friendship bracelets and lanyards, dream catchers, and nature mandalas but also starting some photography with the older campers.

"Hey you." Kyle reaches out to hug me and plants a kiss on my temple. "So, did you hear back?"

"Not yet, I waited until the last possible moment and then drove here at a dangerous speed."

"Well don't go killing yourself when a photography contract is about to come through!"

That's right. Little ole me, Liz Collins Professional Photographer, was approached by a big lifestyle blog to produce exclusive content for them. They're tired of trying to find photos for each post and using stock photos anyone else could use is bad for their brand. One of their writers, Olive, contacted me after seeing my name on some of her favorite stock photos.

They said they'd email me with the contract by the end of the day and it's now Friday at 3pm so I'm getting anxious.

Well even more anxious. I've been anxious since we first talked last week.

Kyle has settled into Lakeville. He's living on the camp property for now but in a few weeks he's moving into an apartment that's over the hardware store downtown. I'm going to stay with my parents but I expect to be spending most of my time there too.

I kept my job at the coffee shop until camp started and I'll go back there next week. Families are starting to book their portrait sessions for the fall and Kyle keeps encouraging me to actually call myself a professional photographer. It felt so good to say it. So good that I stayed up late and built my website. Which is how Olive found me.

My phone rings and when I look at it Nora's face is on the screen. Kyle gives me a chin nod to say it's fine for me to take it.

"So? Are you a contracted photographer yet?"

"Ha, hey Nora. No, not yet. Haven't gotten the email and now I'm at camp so my internet connection is shoddy at best."

"Go home then! Make Kyle do his own damn job." I freaking love her.

"Maybe I will." I turn and watch Kyle interacting with a family picking up their camper. He's so relaxed here in nature and his chill vibes spread to those he works with. I thought he was stoic in the city but Forest Kyle has City Kyle beat.

"Okay, but that's not the only reason I'm calling." Nora says, interrupting my thoughts of Kyle.

"No?"

"No. I'm calling because. Well," she pauses, for dramatic effect but it's working on me. "How do I say this?"

"Spit it out!"

"Geesh, take a chill pill Liz."

"Sorry."

"It's fine. Okay, now where was I? OH yes. That's right. I'm in love."

"I'm sorry what? With who?" Nora has been on a dating spree and I honestly can't recall the name of the last guy she talked about.

"His name is Harold." Nope, doesn't ring a bell. "And he's a cat."

That makes more sense.

"You got a cat named Harold?"

"Yes ma'am."

Nora then tells me about how she was walking past a shelter and this old ass cat was just sitting in the window giving her the sink eye, as cats do, but she couldn't look away. Their connection was instant. She walked into the shelter and asked about him. Apparently he's fifteen years old, had lived with an old lady who passed away and no one in her family wanted him. Nora was filled with a sense of injustice for the poor old guy so she filled out the adoption forms right then and there.

Nora's story is taking quite a while to tell and Kyle is looking at me with a question in his brow. I just shrug and go back to listening to Nora describe the different cat toys she's already purchased.

She doesn't even have the cat yet. They have to run a background check.

I'm worried for her mental state if this doesn't go through.

Finally she says she's going to go and cat proof her apartment, whatever that means, and tells me to call her when I hear from the blog. I walk back over to Kyle.

"Everything okay?"

"Nora is getting a cat."

"Ah, I understand." He says as he picks up the papers and heads to the camp office. "Should we get a dog?"

"Who? Us? Like you and me?" I don't think I was able to hide the surprise in my voice.

He chuckles. "Yeah. Us. Like you and me."

"I mean I'm a dog person more than a cat person but I don't know if you're allowed to have a dog in your apartment and there's no way my mom would go for it seeing how she likes to keep the house so tidy."

"Okay, so we'll get one when we're married."

What now?

I stop in my tracks because we haven't talked about next steps beyond him moving into the hardware store apartment. We just freaking started dating again. I mean it's nice to know where his head is at but, what?

"Liz, I'm kidding." Kyle looks back at me and smiles. "I can see your brain churning away and I don't want it to explode. Now, follow me."

Kyle leads the way out the back of the office to a clearing in the campgrounds that have a view of the lake. It is one of my favorite vistas. It's so calming to just stand here and take it all–

"CONGRATULATIONS!"

I squeeze my eyes shut and duck for cover at the sound before realizing people were yelling congratulations. I open my eyes to find my parents, my siblings, Mitchell and Sandy from the coffee shop, and Nora standing together holding up a big sign. I look closer at the sign and realize it's my name and photography logo on a banner. I turn towards Kyle who is standing next to me.

"You got the contract. And we got you a studio in town." He says matter of factly.

"What? What!" What is happening right now? "Ohmigod. Ohmigod." Tears are forming in my eyes as my gaze bounces from person to person in front of me.

"We're so proud of you Lizzard," Dad says while stepping forward. "When Kyle told us about the contract you were offered we put what was left from your college savings fund into a small business account for you."

"And we got you a deal on the empty space next door to the shop!" Sandy shouts from her place at the end holding the sign.

"I looked over the lease and got everything squared away." Margaret says.

"And, I was responsible for keeping the internet unplugged at home." Charlie Jr says, oddly proud of himself for that task.

"My job was to distract you, but Harold is 100% real." Nora says with the biggest smile on her face. "Your boyfriend got us all together to celebrate your success."

I look over at Kyle who is standing with his hands in his pockets. A sheepish smile on his face like he didn't just organize the biggest surprise of my life. When I think back to where I was a year ago it felt like nothing in my life was worth celebrating. I was forcing myself into a life I thought would make people proud of me. I've learned that doing what brings me joy makes the people who love me proud. Which brings them joy too. And, Kyle played a big part in helping me realize that.

"Thank you." I say as I step towards him. I throw my arms over his shoulders and he brings his hands to my waist, swaying me side to side as we embrace.

"You're welcome. Congratulations Liz," he whispers to me as our foreheads meet.

Knowing my family is right behind me I don't let our kiss get too passionate. That can wait until later. It doesn't stop Nora from yelling out a *whoop* and clapping obnoxiously. It makes me laugh and we break the kiss. Kyle slides his arm around my shoulder and walks me over to the group.

I shake my head a bit realizing that I have a job my family approves of, one that doesn't require a fancy wardrobe, a photography studio which is better than my own apartment, and a supportive, thoughtful, and sexy boyfriend. Everything a girl could ask for.

THE END

ACKNOWLEDGEMENTS

Someday my acknowledgement section will be full of editors and agents and writing cohort partners. Or maybe I'll be a self-publisher forever. Meh, either way works for me. Here For It was a solitary journey. I started writing it without anyone else knowing for a few months. Then I told Danny, my husband. Then a friend. And then another. And then I announced it to my newsletter readers who welcomed it with open arms and I about died.

But the book wasn't done yet so I kept kickin'.

Danny, thank you for not telling me I was crazy to try and do this. Thank you for the encouragement. Thank you for the inspiration. Thank you for making me laugh during our water cooler breaks. I'll always laugh. Thank you for cooking and for cleaning and, maybe most meaningful, for offering to read it.

Thank you to my friends and family for reading it and for still talking to me after reading the sex scenes (they're fiction but I understand if eye contact feels tricky).

Thank you to my kiddos for the understanding that you need to get your own snacks when Mommy's in the writing zone.

And reader who I haven't met yet, thank you for letting this romance into your world and I hope you enjoyed it.

I will inevitably leave someone off the list. I'll forever be a people pleaser so the idea of missing someone physically hurts. Instead of listing everyone by name know this, if you in anyway talked to me about this book before I wrote this section, Thank You.

Erin Marie Bassett is a geriatric millennial, wife and mother of two living in Chicago. (A mile west of Wrigley Field but she, like her husband and kids, are St. Louis Cardinal Fans). When she's not reading or writing romance, Erin helps small businesses and local organizations use the magic words to connect with their communities. She volunteers hard at her kids school and she believes in the power of S.L.O.W. Living.

Her doctor tells her not to but she drinks a lot of coffee. Like, a lot.

Connect with Erin Online & Sign Up for Her Tuesday Night Newsletter
erinmariebassett.com
@erinmariebassett

Erin's Favorite Read-Them-Over-and-Over Romances

(Which she reads via paperback. She's lost count of all the Kindle Unlimited romances she's devoured.)

Nora Goes Off Script by Annabel Monaghan

Highland Fling by Meghan Quinn

The Vancouver Agitators Series by Meghan Quinn

Portrait of a Scotsman by Evie Dunmore
(And all her League of Extraordinary Women Books)

Rock Bottom Girl by Lucy Score

Emma of 83rd Street by Audrey Bellezza and Emily Harding

One Day in December by Josie Silver

The Twelve Dates of Christmas by Jenny Bayliss

Set on You by Amy Lea

The Dead Romantics by Ashley Poston

Love on the Brain by Ali Hazelwood

Northanger Abbey by Jane Austen

But wait! There's more!

Keep Reading for a preview of *Upstate Expectations*, a new novel from Erin Marie Bassett coming Spring 2024.

(Warning… it's spicy from the start!)

UPSTATE EXPECTATIONS

By Erin Marie Bassett Coming Spring 2024

CHAPTER 1
JIMMY

It hasn't rained this hard in months. We were practically in a drought so I'll be an old man and say I'm glad that it's raining for the plants sake but it is making driving home fucking miserable. My wipers are moving back and forth across my windshield and the sound is drowning out the country station I have on playing the latest Hayes Farrow hit. The wind is gusting and I can feel it trying to blow my truck off the road. I take my foot off the gas for a second to relax my hold on the steering wheel and that's when I first see the flashing lights.

Someone's hazards are on about 100 yards in front of me. I would hate to be stuck in this and I would hate myself more if I could help but didn't stop. I pull my truck off behind the little black sports car, put on my own hazards and step out to see what's going on.

I can see one person in the car ahead of me but the rain makes it difficult to see clearly. I can't tell if it's a man or a woman. As I get closer I see a swish of long blonde hair like it's being flicked over a shoulder. I come up next to the window and see the back of her head, slim shoulders, and the hem of her skirt that cuts a straight line across her trim thighs. This might just be my lucky day.

I clear my throat, ready to muster my best "How can I help you ma'am" charm, raise a knuckle to rap on the window when she turns and lets out a blood curdling scream.

"OHMIGOD! NO! I'm poor! I'm skinny! Definitely not a good snack!" She yells through the window. Even through the glass it is muffled but I can clearly hear what she says.

She thinks I'm going to murder her and eat her.

"Ma'am, open up, I am not going to murder you. I have snacks in my truck."

She cracks the window an inch. I see her holding a pen in her hand like a slasher knife.

"You have snacks?"

I laugh. "Yeah, snacks, a blanket, and a cell phone charger."

"And you're not going to murder me?"

"No ma'am."

She rolls up her window and I honestly don't know what to expect next. I'm waiting there when she suddenly opens the door and it slams into my legs.

"Fuck!" I yell out.

"Oh shit, I'm sorry! I thought you moved. Took the old car door right to the junk huh? Sorry about that."

"Not to the junk, to the knee." I correct her even though I'm wincing in pain.

"Ah, good then, knees can be fixed." She closes the door and I am flooded with the smell of her perfume as she walks past me to the trunk. She pops it open and grabs a wheely suitcase with leopard spots on it. She pops the handle and starts walking to my car. That's when I notice the high heels.

Seriously who is this chic that is 10 miles out of town on the only road leading in and out? Lakeville is pretty close knit so we know not only the other people who live in town but the people who visit them regularly. I can say for certain I've never seen this blonde before.

She's twenty steps ahead of me as she continues to click clack towards my truck. She must hit the button on her key fob because behind me her car lock beeps. I jog to catch up to her and take the suitcase out of her hands. She mutters a tentative thanks and follows me to the passenger side.

I open the door for her and she just stands there.

"Up you go." I say in a teasing tone.

"Ugh, actually."

"What's the matter?"

She pauses, and then hikes her pencil skirt up her thighs so she can hop up on the runner and slide into the seat. My jaw about hits the floor as she gives me a view of her thighs only leaving about an inch to go before I'm sure some lacy panties would be found.

I swallow hard, shut her door, and then pop her suitcase into the backseat. I make my way around to the driver's side door and climb in.

"I don't know what kind of small town weirdo you are but I will tell you this. Be sure to fuck me before you murder me because I'm great in bed." She says as she buckles herself in.

"Ma'am, I'm not gonna murder you. I'm just going to try and get you to safety in this storm."

Lighting cracks just ahead of us and the thunder rumbles immediately. She lets out a little yelp next to me. I know better than to be a sitting duck in a lightning storm so I turn the car on and put it in drive.

The AC is blasting which makes my nipples stand up straight in my wet tshirt. I chance a glimpse over at the girl in the front seat and notice that her nipples are pointing up and pressing against her silky top.

I clear my throat. "So, where ya headed?"

"Umm, I'll have to wait for my phone to charge a bit to get the address."

"What town is it at least?"

"Lakeville, we're not far."

"Yeah I know Lakeville." Interesting, so she's visiting someone in town. I haven't been home in a week but I have a feeling I would have heard about a cute redhead moving in.

I drive slowly because the 10 miles to town will go by quick and if her phone is totally dead we might need some time for it to recharge. She's sitting straight as a rod, her hair damp against her head. She's cradling her phone in her lap looking down at it and her knee is bouncing up and down nervously. I look back up at her face and she's biting her bottom lip in worry.

"So I should tell you that even though I don't know where I'm going and I've only ever been here once before my friends Liz and Kyle are expecting me and they're probably worried sick. Like they'll be calling the sheriff or whatever you townies use for law enforcement."

"Yeah, we townies respect Joseph, he's the sheriff. Has been for twenty years. Good fella. Always volunteering his time. And his wife makes a delicious apple pie."

Honestly I have no idea if Susan makes apple pie but this girl seems to think I'm a country bumpkin so I'm leaning into it a little bit. She did say she's been here once before and that she's visiting Liz and Kyle. I went to school with Liz, I've known her all my life and Kyle is her fiance who moved here when the foundation his Aunt runs started operating the camp just outside of town. He's a good guy, we've got out fishing together a few times and have hung out at bonfires.

And I know exactly where they live but I don't feel like sharing that information with the city slicker sitting in my front seat.

"Your friends will be able to bring you back to your car in the morning. You're about 10 miles outside of town." I'm just trying to be helpful.

"Oh, good. Okay. And I guess they'll have gas, or there's a tow truck in town? When my phone died I figured I was close enough but then the gas tank just kept getting lower and lower and the storm kept getting stronger so I pulled over. The whole time I was just envisioning the headlines. City Girl Gets Abducted On The Side of the Road. Friends Say She Was One of a Kind."

She's one of a kind all right.

"And I should not have been listening to that murder podcast while driving upstate by myself but they're just so interesting! It's part of why my phone died so not only did I lose my GPS I didn't get to hear where they found the girl's body. I'll have to catch up with it tomorrow even though Liz hates that shit. She's such a goody too shoes sometimes. I mean, don't get me wrong, the girl can party, but once she called me after Kyle put his finger in her butthole while doing her from behind and she was shocked that it would feel good. I mean c'mon girl! Everyone knows that's the second best orgasm a girl can have. The first obviously being when-- YAHTZEE! My phone is back on. Okay. First things first, GPS."

What is happening? Who is this girl? And what is the best kind of orgasm a girl can have?

"Now I'm dying to listen to the podcast again, oh, ha, get it, dying? But since you haven't heard any of it yet I'll wait. You really have to let the tension build before getting to the climax."

Does she know she's turning me on with the way she talks?

"Oh, GPS says we're a minute away. How'd you do that?"

"I know where Liz and Kyle live. I live in Lakeville too."

"Oh, well you could have just said so."

"I was interested in hearing you talk."

I pull up in front of the house, put the truck in park and turn off my lights. They're in a cul de sac and their neighbors don't need my headlights shining in their living room.

Lightning cracks again and she visibly startles. She takes a deep breath and turns towards me in her seat. It's dark in the truck and even though I can't make out the details very well I can tell she's a beautiful woman.

And her nipples are still pressing against her shirt.

She extends her hand to shake. I grasp it in mine and, shit you not, lightning flashes outside and electricity shoots through my bloodstream. We're frozen looking at each other in the dark.

Suddenly she launches herself towards me and I barely catch her by the waist before she's straddling my legs. Her skirt pulled all the way up above her ass. She leans in and plants a kiss to my lips and I respond by grabbing her ass and pulling her down onto the erection that started to build when she mentioned orgasms a few minutes ago.

She lets out a little whimper as she rolls her hips over me. She's clutching my jaw in her hands and keeping her mouth pressed up to mine, she breathes in through her nose spurring me on. I test her kiss by letting my tongue pass my lips and am rewarded for my bravery by her opening her mouth and our tongues dancing against each other.

Lust shoots through my entire body. I have no idea who this woman is but this is easily the sexiest moment of my life.

I drag my hands up her back, feeling her warm, damp from the rain skin against my fingertips. I reach her ribcage and spread my hands across her sides. My thumb just an inch from the bottom of her breasts. Expecting this to end at any moment, and not wanting to push my luck, I stay right there, slowly caressing the skin under her tits with my thumbs.

She moans and arches her back forward which puts her tits up against my chest.

"Please." She whispers.

I don't recognize the grunt that comes out of my mouth after her request but I move my hands up to her breasts and cup them. I can feel her nipples through the delicate lace. I curl my hands around her and the feel of her soft flesh under the fabric is incredibly hot.

My cock is painfully pressing against my jeans at this point. She starts to rock against me. Her hips roll back and forth in a salacious rhythm as I massage her tits.

I don't think I've dry humped a girl since high school but that's exactly what's happening in my truck right now.

She breaks the kiss and presses her hands into my shoulders, she throws her head back and her wet hair slaps against her back. She grinds harder and I feel my balls tighten.

Fuck I'm going to come in my jeans.

She leans forward and presses our foreheads together, still riding my lap. I move my hands back to her ass and hold on tight. Her breathing gets more shallow and little whispers of "yes" escape her lips.

She inhales a succession of short breaths before letting out a squeak as her legs stiffen and squeeze in. Shit, she's close.

I slide myself down a few inches in my seat which gives her direct access to the bulging fly of my jeans. She scoots forward and lets herself go.

It's still dark in the cab but I can see the tension in her face melt away as she comes. She slows her hips but stays pressed against me. Seeking out the last bit of friction for herself.

It's on the smallest roll of her hips that my stomach bottoms out and I know I'm about to come. I move my hands to her hips and slowly roll her again over my dick.

Once.

Twice.

Third time's the charm.

My cock swells and my orgasm rips through me leaving my legs numb.

She takes a deep breath.

I do the same.

I look up at her and see a fire in her eyes that I'm sure is matched in mine.

She opens my door, slides off my lap and out of the truck. She closes the door and walks around the front to get her bag. She opens the door, grabs her bag, and in the sultriest voice I have ever heard she says, "Thanks for the ride," before closing the door and walking up to the house.

I pull my hand down my face and blink a few times.

Who the fuck was that?

What just happened?

How can I make it happen again?

CHAPTER 2
NORA

"Ohmigawd, I feel like a Jane Austen character."

"It's not that bad."

I give my adorable but clearly suffering from heat stroke best friend a look over my sunglasses. We're sitting in her screened-in porch in the blistering upstate heat after a storm knocked out the power last night.

The same fucking storm that got me stranded on the side of the road. Which I reacted to by dry humping a hottie in a truck.

I've been told I use sex as a deflection or validation tool. But my therapist doesn't know shit. I dry humped that guy as a way to thank him for stopping and taking me to Liz's. That's all.

Definitely wasn't chasing an orgasm to make me forget about my problems.

Nope. Not this girl.

Liz picks up her hand fan again. Now if we actually were one of JA's characters that fan would probably be delicate lace with a little ribbon for keeping it safely around our gloved wrists. But we're not. The best we could do was to make a folded palm style fan out of a cereal box.

Cereal that we had to eat without milk because Liz didn't want to open the fridge again.

Dry cereal, people.

That was my breakfast.

Heat, humidity, dry cereal, and thinking about last night has me feeling sweaty and cranky and I don't see any way it can get fixed without air conditioning.

How Liz can just sit here and act all chill like her thighs aren't melting into the patio furniture I'll never know.

"It is that bad. All we have are room temperature drinks, books, and board games. No music on in the background, just the disturbing hum of cicadas that are seriously creatures of the underworld."

"Wow," Liz says while shifting in her chair to square her shoulders at me. "Nora, I know you weren't a morning person but you've become a bonafide city snob! You came up here to visit me and Kyle and spend a week away from the job that, and I quote, 'is crushing your soul' and now, not even 12 hours in, you're complaining and moping instead of just enjoying this beautiful day."

I stare back at her silently and I can tell she think she won. That I'm sitting here contrite and contemplative.

Wrong.

I'm stewing.

Emotionally and physically.

"You're right," I slyly concede, I catch her smile, "I am a city snob. But you know what? I'm proud of it. And you would have been too if you didn't just up and leave three years ago!"

"That's not fair. You know that's not how it happened." She's right, I do know, and I feel a little bad for saying otherwise. "I couldn't be happier here. Don't take your discomfort out on me. I won't be dragged down by it."

With that, Liz stands up and walks back into the fires of hell. I mean the house. And, maybe I was a little harsh there. Okay probably a lot harsh. It wasn't her fault that the firm I work for, Fosters & Associates, totally dicked her over with a job offer. Liz is a creative type, a little clumsy and completely lovable. She, Kyle, her fiance, and I met as interns. Even though we live a few hours apart we talk every Monday night on facetime. She's got a fiance and now they're happily shacked up in this volcano adjacent mid century ranch.

I haven't found another good girlfriend in the city. Liz would never move back but I miss her and I want her back there with me. Well, that is if I go back.

Up until a week ago, I was killing it. I help major universities raise money from wealthy as fuck donors. I went to college on scholarship so when I get someone to pay it forward I am rewarded knowing I'm helping another Nora Heely from blue collar New Jersey attend an Ivy League school.

But on Friday last week my cat, Sir Harold of Manhattenshire, died. He's been in my life for five years. The longest relationship I've ever had. And he just up and kicked it with no warning. I woke up yesterday morning and he didn't.

I had a meeting with a prospect for a major donation to Cornell at

10am. So I wrapped Sir Harold up in a towel and made room for him in my freezer. I cried while I showered, cried while I tried to put on makeup, and cried in the cab to the meeting.

When I got there, my client's eyes about doubled in size when he took in my appearance. We were ushered to our table where an old woman was already seated.

She was in a Chanel coat, pearls, red lipstick, classic uptight New York widow. I sat down next to her, introduced myself as a consultant who works closely with Cornell and when she held out her hand to shake mine I noticed a cat charm on her bracelet and I broke down.

Wailed.

She was very kind and asked me what was wrong and without thinking I told her the entire store of Harold and I. How I made eye contact with him through the window of the shelter. How he snarled at me. How I knew we had to spend the rest of our lives together. How I shopped for cat toys before the adoption was even approved.

Dave, the rep from Cornell, sat patiently through all of this. After I got the story out, Darlene, the prospect, patted my hand and said, "Ah dearie, we all have the pets we love. Mine was Princess Allegra, she was a rescue as well. Got her right after my Jonathon died."

We smiled at each other and Dave got the conversation directed towards her donation to the school. Things were going well but when Dave asked if we could draw up the paperwork she hesitated.

She looked at me. I froze.

"On second thought, I think my money could be better used by an animal shelter like the ones Harold or Ally came from. What was the name of it again?"

Not wanting to be rude, I told her.

By noon on Friday I was put on a leave of absence for "Conflict of Interest" because I used a prospect for one of Foster's clients for my own personal gain.

Not what happened.

Well, not what I intended to happen. I was just a grief stricken cat lady who still went to work instead of taking a day off.

I called Liz, shared about Harold, and told her I was going to take some time off. I asked if I could come up to Lakeville.

And here we are.

Liz steps back out onto the porch. "Okay, let's go."

I look up at her and she's wearing sandals that look like they're made for hiking and she has a bag slung over her shoulder.

"Where are we going? Mr. Darcy's house?"

"Nora, you know that isn't walking distance from here." She deadpans.

"Ugh, fine but as much as I want to be Eliza Bennet, let the record show I am not *fond of walking*." I say in my best Kiera Knightly impression.

"Noted. Let's go."

I slip on my platform slides because they're the only non-heeled sandals I brought. My current wardrobe doesn't really scream *comfortable for small town excursions*.

Luckily it's only a few blocks to get to the coffee shop in town. The one where Liz works when she isn't being the best photographer in a 500 mile radius.

A little bell chimes as we step in and even though there isn't air conditioning, the coffee shop has ice.

I never thought an iced coffee would taste so good. I take a small sip through the straw, trying to pace myself, and a satisfied moan escapes my lips.

"Was that good for you?" a husky voice behind me asks.

I spin and find myself staring in the broad chest of a man. Slowly I pull my gaze up to his face and whoa mama.

A square jaw covered in scruff that could be on purpose or just what happens when town loses power and you don't shave. Full lips that are curved into a small smirk. And sparkling brown eyes with hints of gold throughout. He's the type of guy that I would definitely approach at a bar in the city if he didn't approach me first.

But in the city he'd be in a suit, no tie, the first few buttons undone to show off his man cleavage. Instead the man in front of me has a washed out green henley shirt on, the sleeves fitting tight around his biceps.

I take a small step back because he's definitely in my personal space and that's when I realize who it is. This is *the* guy. The one who gave me a ride last night. Who got me off while dry humping and instead of the experience being super lame it was super hot.

Since I'm only here a week and we've already hooked up in a sense, I decide to be the flirtatious main character of my story. I smile, knowingly up at him and say, "It's good but I can think of better ways to start my day."

Good line right?

Satisfied, I start to walk away. Leave em wanting more as they say when he chimes back in.

"Me too, but usually that requires you being in bed with me."

I'm sorry, what now?

Who says stuff like that out loud?

To strangers?

Okay, not quite strangers but still!

I thought city boys moved fast but they've got nothing on this guy. There's a playful glint in his eyes and I'm not going to let one comment throw me off my game.

Think, Nora, think.

Oh, I got it.

"Usually? I would think that's the only way."

"Well no," he leans in closer to whisper in my ear and all my senses are overloaded. "There's always the shower, the wall, the counter, my truck. Plenty of places to have a good time."

I think my iced coffee with a splash of almond milk has turned into cement. I am absolutely frozen in place. Mentally my mind is envisioning sex in all those places. With him. Physically my body is reliving the sensations of what we did together last night. Chills are racing down my back from his breath near my ear while, yes, it is hotter than hades here the chills are making me flush instead of shiver.

I know it is my turn to speak but I can't manage to get a full breath.

He pulls back, stands up straight, smiles, and tips an imaginary hat before walking away.

Ladies, his backside is just as nice as his front side.

Noticing that isn't helping the chills slash flush slash wet cement feelings I'm working through.

"I see you met Jimmy," Liz says as she walks over with a pastry bag.

"Ha, um yeah, I guess I did." I blink a few times.

"You okay?" Liz is looking at me like I might actually have heat stroke. And who knows, maybe I do. Aren't the symptoms shortness of breath (check), racing heart (check), flushed cheeks (check), throbbing between your legs (check).

Okay maybe WebDOC doesn't list that last one but they should.

I'm still looking out the front window of the coffee shop at Jimmy's retreating figure as he crosses the street. He does this little skip jog thing that I am surprised to say is sexy. He unlocks his truck and gets in.

In my truck.

Gulp.

Condensation from my iced coffee falls and hits my foot which brings me back to the present. I turn to see Liz is watching me with an amused look on her face.

"What?" I challenge.

"Ooh, nothing."

Don't you hate it when books end?
Same, girl, same.

Visit erinmariebassett.com/books to read
deleted scenes and early, exclusive access
to new work!

take care, talk soon,

www.ingramcontent.com/pod-product-compliance
Lightning Source LLC
Chambersburg PA
CBHW012021110726
47994CB00012B/3262